THE CARESS

A FORBIDDEN BILLIONAIRE-NANNY ROMANCE

RUINED CASTLE
BOOK 4

VIVIAN WOOD

CHAPTER ONE

KEIR

My ex-wife, Kinsley, has leached away everything that I care about. Ever since she had the nerve to show up unannounced, she has wrecked my entire life. And this is her final poisoned gift.

Kinsley has applied for a divorce on the grounds that I am cheating on her. She also included a handwritten note saying that she has evidence of my affair with Ella. The truth is that Kinsley and I were living apart for two years before I ever met Ella.

But in order to tell the court that, I will have to admit that I'm a liar. That I chose to let the public believe that my marriage was intact.

Balling up the court summons in my fist, I rip it to pieces. "Fuck!"

The absolute brass pair of balls on Kinsley... I'm so angry, I'm trembling, radiating violent energy. I feel like an atom bomb seconds before it explodes.

Kinsley claims that she will take my daughter, Isla, even though she hasn't seen her for years on end. Not only that, but Kinsley claims to have video evidence of my fling with the innocent, kindhearted former ballerina Ella. Though there is no law prohibiting me from having an affair with someone as young as Ella, not even my child's nanny, Kinsley knows the press will devour me if they find out.

I'll be a ruined man.

And the worst thing of all was when I had to tell Ella to go back to the States. I had to look her in the eyes and tell her that she should leave Isla and I all alone. The look on Ella's pretty, expressive face will haunt my dreams for years to come. The slight quivering of her lips, the tightening around her eyes.

Even as I said the words, I knew I would regret them. Maybe forever.

At that moment, I knew that I was half in love with the girl that I was asking to leave.

I wake up still thinking about my call with Kinsley.

Not that I think she'll really be able to take Isla away from me. But now, thanks to my stupidity, she definitely has enough money to put up a hell of a fight.

Fuck.

Why did I ever fool myself into thinking my ex would go away quietly? All the years I've spent dealing with her should have taught me better than that. I guess even a jaded cynic like me can get caught up in wishful thinking sometimes.

I scrub a hand down my face as I roll out of bed. My mind immediately goes to Ella and how everything will feel at least a little better as soon as I can hold her in my arms.

Except I can't hold her.

Thanks to Kinsley, I probably won't ever be able to even talk to Ella again without worrying about someone taking a photo of us or using my feelings for her against me.

I look over at the clock on my bedside table. She's probably already gone, but I want to see for myself. There are a million reasons why I can't ask her to stay. I know better than to be seen leaving the apartment with her again, but maybe I can at least say goodbye one last time.

"Why am I torturing myself like this?" I ask in my empty bedroom. I throw on a shirt and some dark slacks, then grab my phone off the nightstand.

Ella probably hates me after last night. I can't blame her. I still regret sending her away like that, but what else was I supposed to do?

The uncertainty is still eating me alive.

Every mistake I make with Ella just gives Kinsley more ammunition to use against me. On her own, I don't think she has a very good case for custody of our daughter. But the longer my name stays in the headlines, the better she looks in comparison.

I've barely taken a step out of my bedroom when I see her door swing open at the opposite end of the hallway. She freezes in place as I move toward her.

"Ella, I'm sorry about last night." Now that I'm closer, I can see her eyes are red and puffy. "I don't want us to part on bad terms," I say, my heart hurting as I reach out to her.

She dodges my touch, then bats my hand away. "Please just leave me alone. I don't know what kind of game you're trying to play right now, but you've already made this hard enough for me."

I deserve this brush-off, of course, but that doesn't make it any easier to accept.

"This isn't what I wanted," I say, still holding my phone with one hand while I shove the other one into my pocket to keep from reaching out for her again. "I never wanted to upset you. Ever."

I've prepared myself for the anger I can see in her eyes, but it's mixed with a raw, fresh pain that I honestly didn't anticipate. Seeing that pain up close and hearing it in her voice cuts me to the core.

3

"Please move out of my way," she says, using her suitcase as a shield to get past me in the narrow hallway. "You're the one who told me to leave without any warning. This is all happening because of you." She huffs out an irritated breath when I don't immediately step aside. "What do you want, Keir? We're done. You said it yourself. You obviously don't care about me or my feelings, so why are you pretending right now?"

Anger bubbles to the surface. not at Ella, but at the whole situation. Kinsley really fucked up my whole damn life. I open my mouth to try to express my thoughts, but my phone buzzes in my hand before I can answer. It buzzes two more times as I start to shove it into my pocket. Mostly out of reflex, I look down at the screen.

"Oh, shit." My breath catches as I skim the incoming texts. Each one is from a different person, mostly journalists sniffing around for a scoop. Unfortunately, all the texts match the news headline that's scrolling across the top of my screen.

Wendy Alan, a reporter, was killed in an apparent hit-and-run. Authorities haven't named a suspect at this time. Authorities want to question billionaire newspaper magnate Keiran Grayrose.

My mind is racing.

What are the odds that Wendy Alan and her partner Max just happened to die in almost the exact same way?

It's rare and tragic enough for someone to get run down by a car in broad daylight, but for it to happen twice? in two related incidents within such a short amount of time?

No.

This isn't a coincidence. It isn't just a tragic accident. I'd bet half my fortune that whoever killed Wendy is the same person who murdered Max.

My phone is still vibrating with incoming texts, but I don't have time to read or reply to any of them right now. Ella pushes past me while I am distracted by the news, her foot-steps echoing in the grand entry room. I can already hear the elevator doors opening in the foyer from where I'm standing.

"Ella, wait!" I call out, running toward the front of the apartment. "Don't leave yet! You need—"

"Too late," she answers from the elevator. She's watching me and shaking her head, one hand still clinging tightly to her suitcase as I hurry to catch the door. "I'm leaving because of you, Keir. We're finished, just like you said."

The elevator door closes right in front of me as I slide across the marble tile.

"Damn it all." I bang my fist on the closed door, but it's too late.

I want to talk to her, to at least make her understand that I'm not the cold-hearted asshole she thinks I am. But now I have another reason to delay her trip to the airport. A real reason

With so much going on at once, my brain has been strug-gling to make sense of Wendy's death. Now, standing here alone in my quiet penthouse, the pieces are finally starting to fall into place.

Wendy knew about the sex tape. She threatened to expose me. The same way Max threatened me before he was killed.

Everyone who knows my secret is turning up dead. Who else knows?

James.

Kinsley.

Ella, of course.

"Ella," I pound on the elevator door again, despite the fact that I know she's long gone. That uneasy feeling is quickly turning to dread as I jam my thumb against the button to call the elevator back up to this floor. "Come on, damn it all. Hurry. *Hurry*."

It's only been a minute or two since she left, but every

second counts now more than ever. There's still a chance I can catch up to her before she makes it out of the lobby; there's still a chance I can keep her here with me, where she'll be safe while we figure out what to do next.

After what feels like an eternity, I'm finally riding down to the ground floor and silently praying that Ella is still there.

I take off running the moment the elevator doors open in front of me, nearly colliding with a startled group of four slow-moving NewsCorp executives. My personal concierge is leading them through the lobby as I push past the group, sprinting to the front of the building.

"Ella!" I shout, running out onto the sidewalk. I'm too late, though. The black sedan is pulling away with her inside, completely oblivious that her life is in danger.

People are beginning to point and stare at me. There's no doubt in my mind that I'll be showing up in the gossip columns looking disheveled and unkempt as I stand here shouting in front of my building. I don't have time to worry about that right now, though.

Turning and rushing back through the lobby, I take another elevator down to the parking garage. I had hoped to avoid being seen with her at the airport, but that isn't an option anymore.

Her safety is more important than my public image. I just have to hope that I can get to her before anyone else does.

Only once I'm in my car and speeding away from the building do I have the presence of mind to call my head of security.

"Yes, sir?" he answers on the first ring.

My instructions are simple. just three words.

"Glasgow airport. *Now*."

CHAPTER TWO

ELLA

I don't recognize the driver waiting for me in the lobby of Keir's building, but he seems to know who I am.

"Right this way," he says, taking my suitcase and ushering me out to the sleek black sedan idling at the curb. "Is this your only bag, miss?"

I'm too numb to speak, so I simply nod instead. If there's a silver lining to this sad situation, it's that maybe I can finally go back to having a regular, normal life. a life where I don't have to worry about paparazzi or the press. a life where I don't find myself flying across the world at the whim of a moody billionaire.

a life where I don't ever have to see Keir again.

I should probably be relieved, right? I'm in control again. I'm off the emotional roller coaster, hopefully for good this time. So why do I still feel like I could burst into tears at any moment?

"Here you go, miss." The driver holds the door open for me as I collapse into the back seat of the car. "Don't worry." He sneers at the handful of paparazzi who are starting to gather around. "I'll get you away from these vultures."

I nod again and mumble a quick thanks, but I honestly

don't even care. They'll forget about me soon enough once I'm gone. If they really want to snap a few more photos of me looking like a sad, sobbing wreck, I'm not going to stop them.

True to his word, the driver pulls away from the pack of photographers with a speedy aggressiveness that's actually sort of reassuring. For someone who I assume has only been hired to drop me off at the airport, this guy seems to genuinely care about getting me there quickly and without any hassles.

I pick up my phone, half-tempted to text Keir and tell him his normal chauffeur and security detail could take some lessons from the glorified taxi he's hired, but I know he would just reply back with something mean and hurtful. Instead, I sent a quick message to Kaia.

I'll be back in NYC this evening. Dinner?

Her reply comes back within seconds, making me smile and hurting my heart all at the same time.

Oh wow! You know I'm always down for a free meal. Keir is paying, right?

Ugh.

I'm sure the next few days and weeks will be filled with these tiny reminders of the fun times I've had with Keir and the life I'm leaving behind. Knowing I'll have to deal with them doesn't make the reminders hurt any less, though.

Blinking back a fresh wave of tears, I pecked out a reply.

He isn't my man, and he isn't going to be paying for anything else, ever. It's just going to be me and you, like it was before.

Before all of this. Before my life got turned on its head.

Before Keir.

Kaia is kidding, of course. Her husband is one of New York's richest people. There is no need for me to pay for

8

Kaia's food, ever. But it was nice to be able to treat her to a nice lunch on Keir's dime.

The text bubble lights up with little dots to show she's typing, then stops before starting up again a few seconds later. When her reply does finally come through, it makes those tears I've been holding back spill down my cheeks.

You know I'm always here if you need anything at all. I'm glad you're coming home, and I can't wait to see you!

I stuff my phone into my purse and dash at my cheeks. That simple message is enough to let me know that Kaia understands. She knows me better than almost anyone else on the planet. I'm already counting down the hours until I can get a big, sympathetic hug from my best friend.

Yeah, it really will be good to be home again.

I take a deep breath and slowly exhale.

Okay.

O-kay.

I can do this. I *can*. I'm not going to pretend like I won't miss Keir, but this breakup is probably the best thing for both of us if I'm being completely honest.

He isn't ready to commit, and I'm not willing to keep waiting and pretending. not even for Isla, sweet little thing that she is.

God, I'm really going to miss her.

She isn't going to understand why I had to leave so suddenly, and I don't know how Keir is going to explain it in a way that will put her mind at ease. Maybe he'll let me talk to her after a week or two, once things have settled down.

Or maybe she'll understand better than I think. It won't be a problem at all. Her maturity and ability to grasp complex adult issues have already surprised and amazed me more times than I can count. This might just be another one of those times.

"We're getting close to the airport," the driver calls back

over his shoulder, then meets my gaze in the rearview mirror. "Do you need me to make any other stops, or do you want me to just drop you off at the terminal?"

I've been so caught up in my emotions that I haven't even been paying attention to how fast he's been driving or how quickly the city has given way to the suburbs.

"Just take me to the terminal, please," I say, praying I can get myself together before we get there.

It's best that I'm getting all these emotions out now, here in the car, where nobody else can see me. But I won't have this extra layer of protection once we get to the airport. I won't have my own personal driver who will go above and beyond to shield me from curious onlookers and intrusive paparazzi.

For the first time in a long time, I'll be completely alone. And as freeing as I know it's going to be, it's also more than a little terrifying.

I close my eyes and can hear my dad's voice from what feels like a million years ago, when it became clear to me and my family that I really had a shot at being accepted into the New York Ballet.

"You're special, Ella. Your talent and abilities are going to open a lot of doors for you, but there will always be haters and people who don't understand. Those people will try to put obstacles in your path. It's up to you to find ways to overcome those obstacles and thrive."

I remember crying then, too. The prospect of facing my fears alone felt overwhelming, just like it does now. My dad might not have won any awards for parent of the year. God knows he's been putting me through hell lately, but the advice he gave me back then has helped me make it this far. I have to trust it'll help me just as much going forward.

"You're the cream of the crop," he'd say. *"You're the best of the best. You also happen to be a young black woman who*

will be in the public eye. People will be watching every move you make, waiting for you to make a mistake. Some of them will even be hoping you buckle under the pressure so they can cheer at your downfall. You have to be stronger than that. You can't ever let them see you sweat. They can't ever know the emotional toll it takes to be perfect all the time.

I inhale as deeply as I can and hold the breath in, just like he taught me. In my mind, I picture all my stress and all my worries forming into a ball that sits right in the middle of my chest, right inside my lungs.

Slowly, gently, I exhale. As the air leaves my body, it carries all the stress and worries with it. Starting with my head and shoulders, then moving down to my arms and legs before finally reaching my fingers and toes, I'm forcing myself to relax. to calm down. To *breathe*.

By the time we pull up in front of the airport terminal, I've almost convinced myself that I feel good about getting on a plane and leaving Scotland behind.

Leaving Keir behind.

"Here we are," the driver announces. "I'll just grab your bag, and you'll be on your way."

"Thank you," I say, getting out of the car and following him around to the back, then taking my suitcase and one more deep breath before turning toward the terminal.

The days of being driven out onto the tarmac to a private jet are long gone. Instead, I have to cross three lanes of stop-and-go traffic just to make it to the building where I can check in for my flight.

With a wave, the driver climbs back into the car and drives away, leaving me truly alone and on my own for the first time in months.

"Okay," I say out loud to myself. "Now it's time to be strong."

I take a step off the curb and immediately have to jump

back as a motorcycle speeds past. If not for the last-second sound of his engine revving, I wouldn't have seen him at all until it was too late.

"What the hell?" I call out after him as he turns to look back at me over his shoulder. "You almost hit me!"

He's wearing black clothes and a black helmet, making it impossible to see his face or any other details. Still, it's hard not to feel a little frightened as I imagine him glaring at me from behind his tinted visor.

So much for remaining calm and collected at the airport.

The guy on the motorcycle slows down and makes a quick U-turn in the middle of the lane, nearly hitting the car driving next to him in the process.

I freeze as he revs his engine again.

Oh my God. Is he coming back?

Time feels like it's moving in slow motion as he reaches into his jacket. A sense of dread overwhelms me as I see the morning sunlight glint off the muzzle of a gun.

No.

No.

This isn't just some random asshole who wasn't paying attention to his surroundings. He was *trying* to hit me with his motorcycle. And now he's going to finish what he started.

He's going to kill me.

CHAPTER THREE

KEIR

I'll have almost caught up with Ella by the time we make it to the airport. She's two cars ahead, close enough that I've been able to catch a few glimpses of her in the back seat of the sedan over the past few minutes.

Is she still upset? Still angry?

I keep hoping she'll turn around and somehow see me, even though I haven't quite worked out what I'm going to say when I finally get the chance to speak to her again.

Whatever I'm going to say, it needs to be good. It needs to be convincing. It needs to be enough to make her want to stay, even though I've been an asshole these past couple of days.

She'll have to stay. Her safety depends on it. But I have my jet on standby in case I need to chase her all the way to New York City. Hopefully it won't come to that, but I refuse to let her out of my sight while there's still a murderer on the loose.

Fuck, if I'd only realized how much danger she was in before, I could have avoided all of this. We'd still be sitting in my apartment right now.

Together.

Up ahead, I can see Ella get out of the car. This is my chance. I need to get her attention before she crosses the street to the terminal.

I turn off my car engine and open the door to step outside, not giving a single shit that I'm blocking the traffic behind me. They can wait. If I'm lucky, it'll only take me a few seconds to convince Ella to come back to the apartment with me.

The sound of an impatient jackass revving his motor behind me interrupts my thoughts. I turned to look over my shoulder just in time to see a motorcycle swerve past.

"Fucking bastard," I mutter, raising my hand to flip the guy off, just as I hear Ella's voice call out.

"What the hell?" she yells, a hint of fear mixed in with her angry tone. "You almost hit me!"

Up ahead, I can see the motorcycle turning around. What the fuck is he doing? I start to move past the car that's still standing between me and Ella, then stop in my tracks.

Fuck.

I can see exactly what the guy on the motorcycle is doing now. He's coming back. And he has a freaking gun.

There isn't time to think. "Hey!" I shout, hoping to distract the guy as I start running toward Ella. I need to get between her and the motorcycle.

Nothing else matters.

Ella doesn't seem to hear me, and the guy on the motor-cycle is only focused on her. She darts to the side and starts running as the first shot rings out, but she's running the wrong way.

"Over here!" I yell, chasing after her as she heads straight for the parking garage. She'd be safer in the terminal, but the garage is closer, at least. "Come after me, you fucker," I yell. "Stay away from her."

I'm running as fast as I can and hating that I have absolutely no control over what's happening right now. I'm too far away to help Ella and too damn slow to stop the crazy bastard who's chasing her.

She ducks and weaves through the rows of parked cars, leaving the guy on the motorcycle behind.

Perfect.

If he can't get to her, he'll have to deal with me.

He turns to look back at me, then points the gun in my direction. "Shit," I mutter, diving for a concrete pillar just as a bullet whizzes past the space where my head was. Another bullet ricochets off the pillar, making me wince even though I know I'm relatively safe at the moment.

It's quiet in the garage.

Too quiet.

"Come over here and get me, you son of a bitch," I yell again, but there's no response. The only thing I can hear is the sound of his engine and my own thundering heartbeat. "I'm the one you're looking for," I say again. "Not her. I'm right here waiting."

To hell with this!

I can't keep hiding back here when I know Ella still needs me. I peek around the corner and see the motorcycle a few yards ahead, still running. But the guy is gone.

Moving from the pillar to crouch next to the nearest car, I can see him walking slowly from row to row, his gun drawn and ready to fire. He's hunting her like she's his fucking prey.

So now I need to get to him before he finds her.

As quietly as I can, I hurry from car to car, keeping my head low in case he turns and starts shooting at me.

We've made it to the end of the row, where the shooter and I spot Ella at the same time. She's limping away as fast as she can, but it isn't fast enough.

He starts to aim the gun, and I see red. I run toward him at full speed, my body colliding with his just as he fires in Ella's direction. "Fuck you," I growl, grappling with him and trying to pin his wrist as we hit the ground. "I won't let you hurt her."

I'm so worried about the gun that I don't see his other fist until it's too late. Pain explodes in my jaw and makes my ears start ringing as we wrestle for control of the gun.

"Let... go," I shout, a primal rage overtaking me as I slam his wrist down onto the pavement over and over again. It's enough to make him lose his grip. I lunged for the gun as soon as I saw it hit the ground.

His fist connects with my face again, but I don't care. I have the gun. Now I just need Ella.

He's already scrambling toward her as I level the gun and try to aim. My jaw is throbbing and my vision is blurry from the second punch, but none of that shit matters right now. If I can just buy her some time, that'll be good enough.

If I happen to kill this bastard in the process, even better.

I fire at him just before he reaches her. I see him stumble and hear her scream as I stagger toward them. The throbbing in my head is intense. I can taste the metallic tang of blood and adrenaline in my mouth as I aim the gun again.

No, I can't shoot now. Not when there's a chance I might hit her.

He looks back at me with Ella trapped in his arms. I can almost see him weighing his options. I'm only a few feet away, and I'm raising the gun again. I might not be able to fire it, but I can still use it as a weapon to hit him in the head.

With a frustrated grunt, he throws her at me, sending her straight into my arms.

"I've got you," I say, tucking her behind me so I can get a clear shot at her attacker.

"Why is he trying to kill us?" she asks, her whole body trembling as she clings to my side. "Where did he even come from?"

I fire the gun again, but there's no way I can hit him. He's ducking and weaving between the rows of cars. I have to make the choice between chasing him and staying with Ella.

I'm choosing Ella.

"I don't know," I finally answer as I wrap my arms around her. "But you're safe now, okay?"

"You got him earlier." You shot him just before he got to me, but he just kept coming at me. "Like a... a monster." She collapses against me, sobbing. "Why, Keir? Why is all of this happening?"

I don't have any good answers. Even if I did, this isn't a good time or the right place.

"Let's go," I say instead. "We'll talk later." I promise."

My word probably doesn't mean much to her anymore, but it's the best I can do for now. At the very least, she's alive and well in my arms.

I came way too close to losing her this time.

CHAPTER FOUR

ELLA

I feel like I'm running through a nightmare, and everything is a blur. I've almost been run over and shot. I've lost my suitcase. And now?

Now Keir is somehow here with me, and I'm in his arms, sobbing uncontrollably. which, for the record, is the last place I would have wanted to be if someone had asked me just a few minutes ago.

I don't know who the crazy man with the gun was or where he went. I don't know how Keir managed to appear out of thin air just when I needed him the most. I don't know if I'm going to be able to catch my flight now that I've almost been murdered in the airport parking garage.

All I know for sure is that it feels impossibly, embarrassingly good to be back in Keir's arms right now. He risked his life to save mine. Even though I'm more grateful than I can possibly express in words, I also have a lot of questions.

Questions he doesn't seem to want to answer.

"Let's go." He takes my hand and starts to lead me from the parking garage. "We'll talk later." I promise."

I wince as I try to walk on my injured leg. Keir immediately stops, supporting me with his body as his expression changes from angry to worried in the blink of an eye.

"What happened?" He looks me up and down as if he's seeing me again for the first time, inspecting every inch of my body and making me feel unusually vulnerable even though I'm fully clothed. "Did he hurt you? Fuck, were you hit by a motorcycle or a bullet or—"

"No," I interrupt, hating myself just a little for enjoying the way he seems to suddenly care about me again.

I can't get weak now, though. I have to stay strong. He's the one who kicked me out of his apartment and sent me off to catch a flight back to New York.

Not that I blame him for any of the craziness that just happened, of course, but it wouldn't have happened at all if we were still sitting up in his penthouse together.

Just saying.

"I'm okay, I think," I continue. "I honestly don't know what happened, but I know he didn't run over me or shoot me. It might just be a pulled muscle or something from when I dove behind one of those cars earlier."

Before either of us can say anything else, two large SUVs come careening around the corner. Keir's whole body tenses up next to me, and I grip his arm with both hands as a fresh round of terror hits me.

"What's happening?" I ask, trying and failing to get my fear under control as the vehicles pull up in front of us. "Is it the guy? Is he back?"

"It's okay," he says, still holding me close even though I can feel some of the tension starting to leave his body. "These guys are on our side. It's my security detail. I called them earlier and told them to meet me here."

Oh, my God! I feel like I might throw up. My nerves and emotions are frayed to the breaking point. I seriously can't handle any more surprises.

"It's okay," Keir repeats, helping me hobble over to the door of the nearest SUV as three giant muscleheads pile out and surround us. "They'll take us to my jet that's standing by on the runway. We can hide out somewhere far away from here. Somewhere safe from the media and from gun-toting lunatics."

"Wait, what?" I stop him just as he's trying to half-lift, half-push me into the backseat of the vehicle. "I'm not going anywhere with you. I appreciate you helping me just now, but I'm going home. To Manhattan. Today."

His face falls, and the bodyguards around us start exchanging uncomfortable glances as I brace myself against the door and refuse to get in.

"Come on, Ella," he lowers his voice and jerks his thumb toward the backseat. "Just get in, please." "I already told you we can talk later, once we don't have to worry about getting shot out here in this parking garage."

I actually have to take a second before I reply to make sure I'm not going crazy. Or maybe he's just gaslighting me? Trying to find out exactly where my breaking point might be?

because I'm definitely there. I've reached that point. And if he doesn't stop with these damned mixed signals, I'm going to scream.

I might scream anyway, just to make myself feel better.

"Let's get one thing straight," I say, finally giving in and letting him help me into the vehicle. "This is the last thing I want. I'm only going with you right now because it's too dangerous to stay here in this garage."

"Fine," he mutters through clenched teeth. "We don't have to get along or be happy." "We just have to get out of here."

And God, if that statement doesn't perfectly sum up our relationship, I don't know what does.

Somehow, I muster the self-control to hold back most of my anger and all my sarcastic replies for the next several

20

minutes until we've been escorted from the SUV to Keir's private jet. But once it's just us and the flight crew?

All bets are off.

"What the hell is all this about?" I ask as the plane starts to taxi down the runway. "You'd better be taking me to Manhattan right now, because that's the only place I want to go." Home. *My* home."

"I'd like to take you there," he grumbles from the plush leather seat across from mine. "Believe me, I really would," she said. "I know you don't want to hear this, but you need to stay with me for a while."

He's right. That isn't what I want to hear.

"I can't deal with this, Keir." I use both hands to rub my tired eyes, then shake my head. "Seriously, I can't." I'm exhausted. I'm still upset with you over the way you treated me last night. I'm in pain from being chased around by some crazy guy with a gun. Now you're telling me you're going to hold me here against my will? for my own *safety*?"

I've been trying to hold my temper in check, but I've been raising my voice over the steadily increasing engine noise until I'm finally yelling at him.

"I honestly don't know whether I should thank you or hate you right now, Keir," I continue, still yelling as I stand up from my seat and move to one of the other armchairs across the narrow aisle of the plane. "All I know is that I can't even think straight because you keep throwing me out and pulling me back in every time I turn around. It's exhausting, and I'm sick of it. I really am."

He follows me as I try to get away in the confined space, sitting down across from me again and leaning forward until there's only about a foot of space that separates his face from mine.

"You're angry. I get it," he says, his own voice surprisingly calm even though I can tell by his expression that he's barely holding his own emotions in check. "I can't blame you for being upset after the way I've treated you. It's shitty. I know it's shitty, and I won't try to defend myself right now even though I swear I never intended to hurt you."

He pauses to scrub a hand down his face, and I feel a momentary pang of guilt for the way I've been shouting at him. just a momentary pang, though. He's still treated me like shit over the past twenty-four hours, just like he said. Then again, he's also saved my life.

"What are your intentions now?" I ask, the rational part of my brain taking over again now that I've had a chance to tell him exactly how I feel. "What happens when we land? I don't even know where we're going, Keir. My family is expecting me to come home, and I feel like they need me there. My dad has been acting out, and my sister is sick. I'm stretched really thin right now, mentally and emotionally, so you'll have to forgive me if I don't really give a damn what your intentions might have been before. You've hurt me, Keir. I have to start protecting my heart."

"I understand," he says, nodding. "All I'm asking for is a little more time to make sure you're safe." We'll wait out the inevitable media shitstorm in Malta. I'll bring Isla and Saffron, so you won't be lonely. "And," he pauses before clearing his throat. "And you won't have to be alone with me unless you want to be."

Damn it all.

I can already feel my anger starting to fade. The look on his face and the tone of his voice are enough to let me know he's sincere. And vulnerable. and too damn handsome.

How am I supposed to stay strong and harden my heart when all I really want is to let him take me into his arms? I want everything to go back to the way it was before he told me to leave. I want the two of us to be happy.

Together.

22

But I'm not sure if that's possible anymore. I'm not even sure I have enough strength or patience to keep trying.

"I don't mind being alone with you," I say, breaking the uncomfortable silence. "I'm just tired of being hurt. I'm tired of being angry."

He nods. "I know. And I'm sorry. "I wish I could promise that I'll never do anything to upset you again, but... He takes a deep breath and opens his arms slightly. "For the first time in my life, I'm dealing with things that are completely out of my control. Kinsley, my parents, my brother, this killer I'm doing the best I can to handle it all, but I know I've made mistakes. I'm probably going to make more mistakes as we go, but I'll still be doing my best. That's the most I can promise right now.

It isn't the fairytale happy ending I've been secretly longing for, but it's still something. It's a sincere apology and an acknowledgment that he's messed up. God knows that's more than he's admitted in the past.

"You're still not off the hook for the way you've treated me," I warn, even though I can already feel the walls around my heart starting to crumble. "And this doesn't change anything between us." I study his expression for another moment and slowly sigh. "But I guess maybe I'll stay with you in Malta." I pause again, narrowing my eyes. "For now."

"That's all I'm asking." For the first time since we've been on the plane together, a faint smile spreads across his lips. "For now."

He leans in closer, and I can feel my lips parting as my breath catches in my throat. I'm not even thinking anymore; I'm only reacting as I tip my head back just enough for him to capture my mouth in a strong, insistent, much-needed kiss.

Just like that, my body is ready to forget all about the last twenty-four hours. I'm ready to forget all about the way he hurt me and how I swore I'd never let him get to me again.

Yeah, my body is totally on board with what we're doing now, even though my brain is still demanding that I hold him accountable for his behavior.

But it's really hard to stick to my guns when his big, warm hands are on my body and he's pulling me across the narrow aisle until I'm straddling him on the oversized leather seat.

I'm definitely going to regret this later.

Eventually.

Probably.

I push Keir away. He resists for a second, kissing me harder. But when I break away and move off his lap, he looks at me. He wipes his lip, his eyes dark with desire. I've seen it before.

It's the expression of a sleek panther who is enjoying playing with his meal before he devours it whole.

Gulping, I take a couple of steps back. My pulse is racing. A part of me wants to beg him to touch me, to kiss me. To make me forget the man that tried to kill us.

But I swear to myself that I can be strong. Just this once, I can tell Keir no.

"I have a headache," I blurt out. I flush. "I'm going to… uh… go deal with it."

Turning, I practically flee toward the back of the plane.

CHAPTER FIVE

ELLA

"Am I intruding?"

I look up from scrolling through my phone to find Keir darkening the doorway to the plane's bedroom. Earlier, I retreated here because it was the only place that seemed far enough away from Keir for my own safety. It even has a door that I could close if I really needed.

But now it looks like my choice to be in the bedroom might be sending mixed signals.

I sit up on the bed, clearing my throat. "What's going on?"

Keir leans in the doorway, just two feet away from me. I could almost reach my arm out and trail it down his muscular chest. I gulp and keep my eyes steady on his.

"Ella." The way he says my name makes it sound like a command. "I think you should ask me to comfort you, sweetheart. I can tell that you want me to."

My eyes widen. My heart jumps into my throat. Still, I hesitate.

What exactly will having sex with him mean?

Keir takes a step toward me, eating up the space between

us. Reaching down to cup my jaw, he tilts my face upward. "Say yes, Ella."

I stare at him, tongue tied, the words already on the tip of my tongue. I'm mesmerized by him. Always have been.

"Yes," I rasp.

He smiles wickedly. "There's a good girl."

Keir steps in the small compartment and closes the door behind him. The door has an ornate mirror on the back that he turns to check out. I can see his face tighten and then smooth out as he makes plans very quickly.

When he turns back to me, he steps to the side, showing me my own reflection.

"Show me how good you are, Ella. Take your dress off," he says, his voice inviting. "I want to see what's underneath."

I flush. "Are you sure that this is a good idea?"

"A good idea?" he repeats. He sticks a finger under his tie and begins to loosen it. "I think I'll die if I don't get you naked soon."

My hands shake. My tongue feels like lead. But there is so much excitement in Keir's eyes that I start to pull my dress over my head. My body feels wooden, almost like it isn't my own. I feel like I'm exposing much more than my skin to him.

I drop my dress to the floor, feeling disconnected from my body. Soon I'm left with nothing but a lacy white thong and a matching bra. Keir draws closer, his eyes hardening as he looks approvingly at my body.

"God, you are so fucking beautiful." He shakes his head, as though he had forgotten until this moment how I look. For a moment, he chews his bottom lip. "Now take off your bra for me, sweetheart. I need more."

He gestures with a flick of his fingertips.

My heart begins to pound. I can't bear looking at him right now, so I sweep my hair back and turn away. It only takes a few seconds to unhook my bra and drag it down my arms. He uses the gentlest, lightest touch on my arms to maneuver me before the mirror.

"I want you to keep an eye on us," he says, his tone a little gravelly. He brushes up against my waist, standing behind me. We both look at the image reflected back at us.

God, we look *good* together. Keir is unbuttoning the top few buttons of his shirt, a wolfish expression in his eyes. He's definitely the predator in this game…

And I'm the willing, sacrificial prey.

I take a glance at the two of us. He pulls me back half a step into his arms. His stiff cock jabs into my back, both promising and threatening good things to come.

Keir's big hands come up to palm my breasts. I feel oddly empowered by looking in the mirror. It's little like watching these hot things happen to someone else. As he pinches my nipples, I shudder. It's strange to be viewing myself right now but I'm surprisingly into it. I gasp and the girl in the mirror gasps… I lean my head back against Keir's chest and step into his welcoming embrace.

"You like the mirror?" he asks. He kisses my ear, causing my whole body to tremble.

"Do that again," I say. I feel him grip my hip as his ear teases the shell of my ear. He nibbles it, which makes me pussy grow damp. "*Fuck*, Keir."

Keir hooks his fingertips in my panties, teasing me. I lean back against him and he skims them down my legs, throwing them aside. The last of my clothes are gone and I'm watching Keir in the mirror with bated breath.

For better or worse, there is nothing between us today.

He holds my hips and takes a step backward to the bed, sitting down. He pulls me down to sit between his knees on a sliver of the bed. The contour of his cock is pushing against my ass cheeks.

In the mirror, I watch as the handsome man maneuvers

the gorgeous girl around. He grabs my knees and divides my thighs, revealing my pussy. That makes me shudder, and it makes my mirror image shudder as well. He kisses my earlobe at the same moment.

His kiss makes my clit pulse. I moan, halfway closing my eyes. It feels so decadent to be doing this here, right now. Joining the mile high club? Yes, please.

"You are stunning, sweetheart." His free hand begins to cup one of my breasts as his hand goes down my body to my pussy.

His deft fingers split my pussy lips and focus on my tender clit. He strokes it with his fingertips, making it throb.

I arch my back and groan quietly. But I never take my gaze away from the mirror. Watching us is way too hot. I can't believe I never thought of trying this before.

"Keir," I say quietly. "We're both so fucking sexy. I don't think I knew how good we looked together."

"We are," he agrees.He presses his lips on a point on my neck, heightening my need. His fingertips spin over my clit suddenly and I practically come out of my seat. "Shhh. Stay with me, sweetheart."

At the same time, he strums one of my nipples. I reach up and place my hand over his, squeezing it to my skin. I'm showing him what I enjoy in the most timid manner possible.

He replies by strumming faster, using the same method I did. His fingers on my clit remain relaxed but they move faster too. He nips my neck a couple times and bites my earlobe.

"Fuck!" I moan, throwing my head back. "Keir…"

I let forth a trembling groan. Keir chuckles, and I can feel the vibrations on the overheated skin of my neck. It's incredibly sexy.

"Do you like that, sweetheart?" he asks.

I attempt to keep my eyes open by nodding. To enhance

the pressure on my clit, I need him to stroke his fingers quicker over my clit. I try to force my pussy into his touch by angling my hips.

He makes a quick sound of rebuke. "Ah ah. You're a grown woman. I want to hear you tell me what you want, sweetheart. Trust me, it'll get you what you need much faster."

It's not what I wanted to hear. I open my eyes, shooting a glare at him for not being able to read my mind. "Faster. Harder. Just touch me, for fuck's sake," I whine.

As he leans us both back a few inches, my hips begin to gyrate. With his free hand, he directs my attention to the mirror. "Watch yourself, sweetheart. Play with your nipples."

The pressure of his fingers on my heated pussy is precisely perfect from this viewpoint. He begins to move his fingers more quickly, spreading my wetness with his fingertips.

"Oh fuck," I say, breathless. "That's so hot."

"Take a look at yourself," he whispers in my ear. "Look at how creamy your pussy is. Look at how you're letting me dominate you right now. Tell me that you aren't about to lose it right now, watching it all play out."

As he says it, I can feel my body getting ready, my pussy getting wetter and wetter. I lean back and half-close my eyes. Nobody else has ever made me feel this hot and naughty, eager for him to make me come.

Nobody has ever come close to making me feel this *desired*.

I try to concentrate on how I'm feeling. My hips feel full and heavy, my breasts are on fire, and my clit practically throbs. I need to come. Not want; I *need* it, like I need air.

"Beg me to make you come," he says into my ear. "I like the way you beg, darling."

Fuck. I can feel it now that I'm getting near. Keir's touch on my clit is almost enough to make me explode.

"Please..." I beg. "Please, Keir."

"Please tell me what?"

I press back against him, attempting to increase the angle of my hips. But he refuses to budge. He simply maintains the same beat, his fingers sticky from my wetness.

"Please, Keir... make me come," I plead.

He moves his fingers quickly, softly shifting our bodies. He just moves his fingers a few degrees but I swear, it's as though he's suddenly striking me with lightening. My hips buck wildly. I come quickly and without warning, my hips twitching, my mouth opening, and a roar bursting from my chest. My orgasm causes my entire body to quiver uncontrollably. Keir simply keeps moving his fingers until I reach down and lay my palm over his, shaking my hand and stopping his movement.

I open my eyes and kiss him right away. Open mouth, a little tongue, and heavy breathing.

Keir turns his attention to me, reaching out to touch my knee. He spreads my knee for a little while, his free hand gripping my opposite hip. My pussy is still fully exposed, and he lightly brushes his palm across my bottom lips.

I shiver, my excitement growing.

"Oh, sweetheart," he groans. He glances up at me, our gazes colliding. "What I'm going to do to you..."

Keir moves, scrambling off the bed. He begins to take off his button up shirt, ripping it off his arms and baring his chest and abs.

He's amazing looking, chiseled as though from granite. He hooks his thumbs in his black slacks and pushes them down, kicking them off. For a split second, he stands naked in front of me, his cock protruding. He's an awesome figure. His expression is intense, his stare is predatory.

It gives me chills. I'm ready for his hands all over my body. Ready to gasp and writhe in anticipation of the pleasure he offers me. I can't wait.

Sitting up, I shudder and grab for him. I draw him down by wrapping my fingers around the solid slab of muscle around his hips. He shoves me onto my back and our legs become entangled.

My air rushes out of my lungs. As he chews his lip, Keir's eyes rake over my face.

"You're so fucking perfect." He says it as though he is mystified before closing in on me and threading his fingers in my hair. "God damn it, Ella."

As he kisses the left corner of my lips, he thrusts against me once. I writhe against his body, gently groaning.

He shifts his upper body weight to his arms, offloading it from mine. I tighten my grip on his waist, biting my lower lip as I glide my fingers down between us. He sucks in a gasp as I approach the tip of his cock, stretching my palm out to delicately touch it.

"God, Ella," he says quietly. He bites his lower lip as he pushes against my fingers. "Do you see just how hard you make me? Hmm? My cock is throbbing for your touch, darling." He leans heavily on one arm, reaching up to cup my jaw tightly. "I'll stretch you out with my big cock. I'm going to fuck you until your pussy creams for me."

My breathing becomes labored. I sense a trickle of yearning escaping from my entrance. I have no question, based on Keir's face, that he means every word he says.

I sigh, feeling impatient, and press my hips against his body. "Don't tease me, baby."

Keir smirks and kisses me on the lips. "Sweetheart, have a little patience."

I raise my brow at him. I slide my hands back and forth between our bodies, touching his cock, which is scorching against even my warm flesh. He hisses and temporarily closes his eyes.

I wrap my little fist around his cock and jack it up and down his length. Growling, he takes my hands and pins them up over my head.

"It's supposed to be about you tonight," he grinds his teeth.

My eyebrows quirk. When I finally speak, I'm a bit out of breath. "This is all about me, Keir. I want to do what makes you happy."

Keir struggles to his feet. He makes a motion to me, his stare like a blazing mark across my nude body. "Sweetheart, come to me on your hands and knees."

I roll over and then push up, turning and approaching him. As I approach, he groans.

"Do you have any idea how fucking hot you are right now?" he grouses.

I come to a halt at the side of the bed, shaking my head slowly. His cock juts out boldly from his body. He takes another step forward, brushing his lower thighs on the bed. I reach out to take his cock, gazing up at him for direction. He shivers as our gazes collide.

I slowly pump up and down the length of his cock. He hisses and brings his hand up to steady mine. He lets me explore for another half-minute before forcing my hand away, his cock in his grasp.

When Keir opens his eyes, his attention is on my mouth. His eyes are dark with hunger and need.

"Open your mouth, honey," he orders. "And put your tongue out. If you want to taste my cock, you'll have to go deep."

I open my mouth and lick my lips. He guides me forward by running his free hand through the mass of my hair. A drop of milky white semen pouring from the head of his cock is the last thing I see before my face is buried against his flesh.

I stick out my tongue, which he prods with the tip of his cock. The skin is as smooth as silk on my mouth and tastes salty and metallic. It is bigger than I remembered. But as soon as I get used to it, he starts guiding my head and lining up my throat using some kind on innate geometry.

Ever so slowly, Keir nudges his cock into my mouth. I try to raise my hand to get some control over how quickly he moves, but he is just as quick to push my hand away.

"Don't," he commands. "You'll just have to trust me again. Can you do that, darling?"

I nod as much as I can, given that my mouth is full of his thick cock. I conceal my teeth and relax as much as I can as I look up at him, my head in his hold. I trust him. He knows just what to do.

Keir thrusts gently for a minute, then adjust the angle of my throat and goes in a little deeper this time. For a second I can't breathe; his big cock blocks my airway.

"Holy fuck," he mutters. "God, right there."

He thrusts again and against, each time looking like he's about to blow his stack. But eventually he takes a step back, popping his cock out of my mouth. I take a deep breath and gaze up at him, breathing hard.

Keir looks at me as he tugs on his cock. "I could do that all night, sweetheart."

"So why don't you?" I ask, my eyes sparkling mischievously.

"Because there are other pleasures, darling. I'm going to taste you first. And then I'm going to fuck you so hard you won't be able to walk right."

Keir's taunt hits me like a jolt of electricity straight to the heart. I can actually feel my pupils dilating. "Is that a guarantee?"

He throws me onto my back and then comes down to settle on top of me. His eyes drink me up. He growls quietly as his fingers travel down to brush my glistening slit.

"You're dripping wet, sweetheart. Almost like you want this every bit as much as I do."

I squirm, licking my lips. "Less talking. More action."

He licks my fluids off the tips of his fingers as he puts his gleaming fingers to his lips. As he tastes me on his hands, he shuts his eyes and lets out a deep sigh. "You're fucking fantastic, sweetheart. Your taste is just like fucking candy."

I know he's waiting for a response to his dirty talk, but I'm having trouble finding the words he's looking for. All I can think of are his fingers, which are now teasing their way along my seam and toying with my clit.

"Fuck," I manage. "Jesus, Keir."

He gives me a deep, hungry kiss. His rock hard cock is digging into me. I groan loudly, my excitement growing.

"Keir," I say quietly, my hands on his shoulders. "Quit teasing me. Seriously, I might die."

"Just take a breath, sweetheart." His voice is low and husky. "I keep getting distracted by your incredible body."

He kisses the corner of my mouth before moving down my body.

I can feel my clit throbbing, and I can imagine how fucking fantastic his tongue will be when it finally reaches my pussy. Jesus, I really want him. He has made me wait so long...

Keir kisses his way down my lower tummy, up to my thighs, and right on top of my pussy. He slides his fingers around my pussy lips, caressing the area. I squirm.

I briefly consider killing Keir and just getting a vibrator instead. But he buries his entire face in my pussy in the next second, feasting on my pussy. All thoughts of killing him vanish into thin air as soon as he flicks the tip of his tongue against my clit.

He swishes his tongue over my clit, knowing exactly what he's doing. He takes my sensitive clit in his mouth, softly sucking and flicking his tongue across my bud.

I groan and clutch my breasts, squeezing them and grabbing my nipples. My hips buck and my back bows, my body beyond ready for this moment.

His tongue swiftly transforms me into a trembling, wailing lunatic. I writhe my pussy against his tongue, unable to keep still, but his firm hands on my hips keep me in place. He licks and sucks till all I see are stars and rockets, and I feel like I'm going to burst.

The strain that had been building up inside of me finally dissipates into a dazzling ball of light. My mind shatters, fragments falling in all directions. I scream his name as I sink my fingers into his shoulders and pull at his hair.

He continues to lick, twirling his tongue. I grab his shoulders and push him away roughly. He has the filthiest grin on his face as he stares up at me.

"Sweetheart, you taste better than I could have dreamed."

He stands up and comes up to kiss my lips firmly. On his lips, I can taste myself.

Earthy, salty, and fulfilling.

There's something dirty and extremely personal about kissing him just after he just went down on me... I can't seem to get enough of it. I groan into his lips and hear a low sound emanating from his throat.

"Don't stop," I say softly against his lips. "If I remember correctly, you said you'd fuck me till I couldn't walk straight."

He shudders as his eyes open. He looks at me with such intensity that I could cry. "I promise, sweetheart. I promise we're getting there."

He pulls me back on the bed, taking his cock and pressing the blunt tip on the inner of my thigh. I draw him in with my legs, causing him to re-adjust slightly till the tip of his length rests on my wet pussy. As he pushes inside, stretching me out with each inch, we both gasp in unison.

My nails sink into his flesh as I hold his shoulders. As he works his way in, his forehead furrows in concentration. As I stretch and accept his gigantic bulk, my pussy clenches.

"Fucking hell," he says quietly. "Your pussy feels amazing, Ella."

I grind my pussy into him as I move my hips. It feels good to rub his cock against my inner walls in different ways. I move my hands down to his ass and grab what I can, wrapping my legs around his body.

"Fuck!! Keir, please. Don't hold anything back from me."

He glances up at me, a sheen of perspiration beginning to form on his brow. Then he moves, gently thrusting his cock into and out of me. I begin to feel pleasure waves, uncertain at first, then increasingly certain.

Keir pinches the nipple of my breast with one big hand. I start moving my hips in sync with him. Little flame licks begin to unfold themselves deep within me, taking my breath away.

Fuck yes. *Fuck yes.*

"God," I groan. I toss my head back in response to his hesitant thrusts. He's being cautious around me, which I don't want. I throw back my head. "Now, Keir. Fuck me like you'll never see me again. Make sure I will always remember this."

He stiffens for a split second before grabbing my hips and pulling me up a few inches. He abandons his tentative rhythm and begins slamming himself into and out of my pussy. For a split second, my eyes expand. He begins to sweat profusely, his perspiration combining with mine in every single spot where my fingers come into contact.

It feels amazing to move my hips in sync with each thrust. I feel obliged to keep up with him, to meet his hips, to wrap my legs around him and bring him in even deeper. I concentrate on it, closing my eyes and reaching for my own breast. Keir grunts, pausing for a split second. He elevates himself and resumes thrusting. He then pushes my hand away, putting his hand between us.

My back bends as he strokes my clit. My hips are becoming heavy and full, with each of his thrusts dragging me closer to the edge of the abyss.

When I come, I can't hold back the wailing scream I release. He lets himself go at the same time, crying out. I tumble down, down, down... and when my eyes finally drift open again, I find myself in Keir's arms.

It's only right that I kiss him passionately for a few minutes before sighing and pulling away.

"Where are you going?" Keir muses.

"I don't really want to stay in bed with you. No offense, but..." I cut a glance over my shoulder at him. "There is no use in us making nice. Right? Am I correct in saying that this doesn't change anything for us?"

Keir clears his throat and sits up. "I hadn't really thought about it."

That's a non-answer if I've ever heard one.

I push myself upright in the bed and wince as a jagged jolt of pain shoots through my injured leg.

"You don't need to get up just yet," Keir says as he reaches for my arm. "We still have a few hours until we make it to Malta."

At least that answers one of my questions. I pull away from him and scan the small, narrow room for my clothes. "I'm going back to my seat up front," I say without looking back at him. "As soon as I can find my panties."

I can feel him watching me as I quickly move around the

room, scooping up my clothes and scrambling to put them back on again. I don't want to fight with him anymore, so I'm hoping he'll let me leave without hassle.

"Are you upset with me again?" he asks. "Did I do something wrong? Because I'm pretty sure we just had a really good time together."

So much for letting me leave without a hassle.

"We did, but..." I turn to face him for the first time and swallow back a wave of emotions that I didn't expect to feel. Seeing the confusion and irritation on his face only adds to my sadness and regret for the situation.

"But?" he prompts when I go silent.

"But I don't want to complicate things between us." It's such an understatement that it would honestly be laughable if I wasn't so miserable.

"Is it really that complicated, though?" He shrugs, making me want to scream in frustration. "I think we both needed that release, don't you?"

Ugh, it's even more frustrating because he's right. Mostly right, at least.

"Maybe we did," I admit. "But we're done, Keir. We've both agreed that we're done. So no matter how much I may or may not have needed that release, I can't keep doing this. I just can't. As far as I'm concerned, we just had breakup sex." *Excellent breakup sex.* "But that was all it was. That's all it can be. There had better be a private room for me when we land in Malta, because breakup sex is a one-time thing. It can't keep happening."

I expect him to argue, or at least try to change my mind. He doesn't, though. He simply nods and says, "Okay. I understand."

Irritated, frustrated tears are welling up in my eyes, but I turn away and finish getting dressed before he can see them spill down my cheeks.

38

He says he understands, but I don't know if he really does. I don't know if *I* do, for that matter. All I know is that I have to get better at telling him no. I have to get better at protecting my heart.

I have to get better at being alone.

CHAPTER SIX

KEIR

It's early in the morning, but the sun is already high in the Maltese sky and blisteringly hot. It always takes my body a few days to acclimate when I travel this far from Scotland, but I have more important things to worry about than a little Mediterranean sweat as I pace back and forth along the short corridor between my room and Ella's.

I keep trying to talk myself out of knocking on her door, even though I have every right to speak to her. This is my family's house. She's still technically on my payroll as Isla's nanny, though that was supposed to end when I made her leave my apartment in Glasgow.

So why am I hesitating outside her door when I could be in there with her, making things right between us?

Because she already told you she doesn't want to make things right.

Fuck.

That annoying little voice in my head is seriously getting on my nerves. It's almost taunting me at this point. Unfortunately, that little voice is also correct.

I know Ella is still hurt and upset. I know she keeps saying she doesn't want to speak to me. But she also keeps opening up to me and inviting me back into her life, at least with her actions if not necessarily so much with her words.

Well, fuck it.

I'm not going to stand out here in the hallway like a scared idiot all day. I'll at least knock and see if she's awake. If she doesn't want to talk, we won't talk.

"Ella?" I knock quietly. "Are you awake?"

"Yes." Her voice is soft, and I have to lean in close to hear it. "What do you want?"

"Can we talk?"

"No."

It's not the answer I was hoping for, but it's an answer nonetheless. And I know I told myself I'd go away if she didn't want to talk, but... I lied.

"Please?" I continue. "I don't want to argue. I just want to apologize and hopefully do a better job of explaining myself than I did yesterday."

It's the truth, but I'm not sure if it matters anymore. There's no doubt in my mind that she really does want to be alone right now. I know it's my fault.

Surprisingly, she opens the door just enough for me to see her beautiful face. Her eyes are red and puffy. not just because she probably hasn't been awake for very long. She's definitely been crying. That's also my fault.

I need to make things right, but I'm not sure how. It feels like my life has been turned upside down over the past forty-eight hours, but how much has really changed between me and Ella?

"Thank you for opening the door," I begin. "I'm sorry about yesterday. And the day before. I'm sorry about all of it, Ella. I really am."

"I know," she says, nodding. "I believe you."

Okay, maybe this is going better than I thought it would.

"Does that mean you've forgiven me?" I ask, pressing my luck. "Can we go back to the way things were before?"

"No."

Okay, maybe it isn't going that well after all.

"I don't know if we can ever go back to the way things were," she continues. "I don't even know if I want to. I appreciate your apology, but I'm more interested in knowing when I can leave."

Ouch.

There isn't even any anger in her voice. That's how I know she's serious. I deserve it, of course, but it still stings.

"It doesn't have to be like this between us," I offer, trying to keep my tone as calm and matter-of-fact as hers. "We don't have to be at each other's throats while we're here. But I'm not going to keep walking on eggshells around you if you're going to be this cold to me."

I regret the words as soon as they leave my mouth. It's impossible to miss the flash of anger in her eyes this time. I can hear it in her voice when she speaks again.

"Let me tell you something," she hisses, jabbing a finger at my chest. "You don't get to tell me how to act or feel, not after the way you've treated me. Not after the way you cut me out of your life and threw me out of your apartment without a second thought. Without even blinking twice."

"I'm sorry." I put my hands up in surrender. "I've already apologized for the way I treated you the other night at the apartment, but I'll apologize again. I'm sorry for that, Ella. I truly am." I shake my head and take a deep breath. It's too late to pretend I haven't let my own emotions get the best of me. "I hope you know after all this time that I'd gladly deal with all the criticism and the flack to be in a relationship with you if it was just myself that I had to worry about. But as long as I have custody of Isla, I have to make sure I'm putting her needs ahead of mine."

A wry smile appears on Ella's lips. "I can't decide if I should laugh or cry. You realize that now, after it's all over, this is one of the only times you've ever openly admitted we were in a relationship, right?"

The doorbell downstairs rings before I can answer. A large part of me is relieved beyond words.

"That'll be Saffron and Isla," I say, turning to walk away before she can pin me with any other awkward questions.

I might have been literally saved by the bell this time, but there's no getting around the fact that she's right. One of my many failings in our relationship was denying that we were in one at all. But again, I had to think about Isla. I had to do what was best to protect her. That means keeping my family's name out of the tabloids as much as possible.

Another thing I've mostly failed at, but at least I tried. That has to count for something, right? Isla and Ella will both understand and appreciate what I've done someday, right?

A stray thought occurs to me. This would all be easier if I could talk to Ella, really make her understand me. Maybe she wouldn't fight me so damn much if I could just explain myself better.

Swallowing, I make a promise to myself. I decide that going forward, I should at least attempt to make Ella understand my side of things so that it doesn't have to be this damn *hard* to accomplish the simplest tasks.

I hurry down the stairs and through the foyer to open the door, where my daughter is waiting for me with a smile as bright as the Maltese sun.

"We're here!" she squeals, launching herself into my arms. "Did you miss me?"

"More than you know, sweetheart," I answer, spinning her around and planting a kiss on the top of her head before setting her back down on her feet. "Where's your Aunt Saffron? Did you leave her on the plane?"

"Right here," my sister says, coming around the corner with three large suitcases in tow. "Can a girl get a hand with all this luggage? Don't you have a butler or something here with you?"

I laugh as I walk over to take a couple of the bags from her. "Just us for now, I'm afraid. Maybe you could have gotten away with it if you hadn't packed like you were moving in—"

The words die in my throat, and my smile instantly fades when I see my mother appear a few steps behind Saffron.

"Mother?" I ask through clenched teeth as if she might be a figment of my imagination. As if I could get that lucky. "What are you doing here?"

She draws herself up and rolls her shoulders back. gives me an imperious look that I know all too well. She came here ready for a fight. "What? No hugs and kisses for your dearest mama? I wish I could say I was shocked."

I cut my eyes in Saffron's direction, but she suddenly seems extremely interested in one of her luggage tags as she slowly inches toward the door.

"And I wish I could say I'm shocked that you've invited yourself out here with Saffron and Isla," I shoot back. I didn't plan on fighting with anyone today, but what can I say? My mother has a special knack for bringing out the worst in people.

"I don't need an invitation," she huffs. "This is my house. *My* personal property. If anyone needs permission to be here, it's you." Her eyes flick past me, then narrow slightly. "You and your nanny."

Okay, now I'm pissed.

Yes, this is technically still my mother's property, but she hates it here. I guess her need to control my life and every move I make outweighed her dislike of this place, though.

"Leave Ella out of this," I growl, glancing back over my

44

shoulder to see Ella and Isla. Saffron is huddled near the door and hanging on every word. Clearing my throat, I throw my sister a pointed look. "There's tons of food in the kitchen, sis. I'm sure you and Isla are tired after your flight."

She nods and reaches for my daughter's hand, but Isla clings to Ella's leg and shakes her head. "I'm not going anywhere without Ella."

"I'll come with you," Ella smiles down at Isla and ushers her toward the door. "Your dad is right. There really is a bunch of yummy stuff in the kitchen." Then, in a playful whisper that masks whatever other feelings she might be having, she adds, "And since he'll be out here talking to your grandmother for a few more minutes, you might even be able to sneak a candy bar or some ice cream before we have lunch."

That was all she needed to say. Isla takes off with a whoop, leaving Saffron and Ella to follow while I turn my attention back to my mother.

"She shouldn't be here," she says before I can get another word in. "You know I think she's a bad influence on my granddaughter." She scowls. "And on my son."

"Yes, mother," I sigh. "You've made your opinion perfectly clear on multiple occasions. We're all well aware of how you feel and what you think."

"And yet you continue to flaunt your affair at every opportunity. It's almost as if you want to be called out in the tabloids and bring shame to our family. It's a miracle you haven't been sued yet."

"Sued?" I grunt, half-turning to go back inside. I was already annoyed to see her, but this conversation is quickly turning that annoyance into anger. "By whom? For what? Are you really threatening to sue me because you don't like one of my employees?"

I don't know why I even bother asking, since I don't care

to hear the answer. Maybe just because I know how much it irritates her when she doesn't have the last word in an argument.

After all, there's no question where I picked up that particular unflattering personality trait.

"Lord help us." My mother casts her eyes up to the sky as if she's actually religious. "Have I really raised such a fool? I'm not the one who will sue you, Keiran. Not over this, anyway. But you really are a damned fool if you can't see the power imbalance between you and that girl you're sleeping with. The fact that you insist on paying her only makes it worse. Mark my words, your name will be showing up in the tabloids with one of those sexual harassment hashtags before you know it."

I'm tempted to ask how long she had to practice before she was able to insult multiple people at once while feigning concern for those very same people, but somehow, I manage to hold my temper in check.

Barely.

"We're done here, Mother," I say instead, "You're welcome to stay for lunch, but I'll arrange for my driver to take you to a hotel this afternoon. I'm not going to be lectured every time I turn around. I'm not going to let you insult Ella at every opportunity, either. If she wanted to sue me, she would have done it already. God knows we've all given her plenty of reasons."

"No," she says, because of course she isn't going to go quietly. It was worth a shot, but I'm not as foolish as she likes to think. I mostly just want to put her on notice that I'm not going to listen to her lies and insults anymore. "I'm not going anywhere. If anyone is going to leave, it'll have to be you. And you can take Ella with you, but I'll be keeping Isla here with me until further notice."

I've started walking back inside, but that threat stops me

46

in my tracks. "Be careful," I warn her, my voice dropping low as I turn to face her again. "You're playing a dangerous game. It's not one you'll win."

"Are you sure about that?" She arches her brow. "You have no friends. Your family is on the verge of disowning you. There's talk of a no-confidence vote at NewsCorp because you've been out of the office more often than not. Who do you really think will come out of this situation looking better? A disgraced man who is sleeping with the nanny? Or a loving, concerned grandmother who just wants what's best for her family?" She lets the words hang in the air for a moment before sweeping past me. "Think about that the next time you want to threaten me."

Fuck.

It's like my ex-wife and my mother are in a competition to see who can be the most devious and disgusting. Right now, I think my mom might actually be winning.

She won't take Isla from me, though.

I'll fight her until the bitter end. I'll expose every lie and every dirty deed she's ever done. I'll ruin her, even if I have to destroy my own reputation in the process.

CHAPTER SEVEN

ELLA

Seeing my sister's face on my phone screen never fails to cheer me up. And I definitely need some cheering up now that Keir's mom is here.

She hates me and doesn't try to hide it. Every look in my direction and every word out of her mouth when I'm around is tinged with that dislike and disdain.

I don't know if it's because my family isn't rich or because I'm not British, or if there's some other reason for her insistence that Keir end his relationship with me, but it's past the point of being annoying. Especially when I didn't ask to come on this trip. I'm just trying to mind my own business and stay alive at this point.

"Hey!" Joy's cheerful voice and infectious smile make me push all my less-than-charitable thoughts about Keir's mother aside. "I've been worried about you. I thought you were going to be coming home soon."

I feel a pang of guilt as I shake my head. "Sorry, I didn't mean to worry you and Dad. There's been a change of plans. I have to stay." I pause, realizing I probably shouldn't tell anyone exactly where I am at the moment. As long as someone out there is still trying to kill me and Keir, it's probably best if I keep things vague. "I have to stay here for a little while longer. Just to sort some things out. Anyway, how are things at home? How have you been feeling?"

"Fine, I guess." Her smile dims a little. "Same as always."

"Have you had a lot of doctor's appointments lately?"

She shrugs. "Not really. No more than usual."

I don't want to pry too much, especially when I'm not there to comfort her in person, but she isn't giving me much information to work with. And then the way her demeanor changed just now when I started asking about her health and her appointments? The more she tries to play it off and act nonchalant, the more questions I have.

How sick is she? Is she even sick at all?

It kills me to think she might be hiding something from me, but I wouldn't put it past our dad to bully her into a situation where she feels she has no other choice.

"I miss you," I say, forcing a smile in spite of all my doubts. "I can't wait to come home and tell you all about the crazy stuff that's been going on here."

Her face lights up again. "I can't wait, either! I miss you, too. Every day."

God, I wish I could scoop her up and bring her to Malta. She'd be able to keep Isla company. I'd be able to watch over both of them and keep them safe.

"You know I'm always here for you, right?" I promised myself I wouldn't pry, but I have to at least let her know she can count on me if Dad really is putting her in an awkward situation. "You can always tell me anything, no matter what. Always, Joy."

"I know." She turns away for a second and nods. I think I can see tears welling up in her eyes when she turns back to the screen again. "I have to go, but I'll talk to you later, okay? Love you."

"I love you, too." The screen goes dark before I can say

anything else. I'm left wondering if I've accidentally made things worse.

I want her to know she can trust me and count on me, but was I actually pressuring her instead? Does she feel like she has to choose between being loyal to me or to our dad?

Maybe I should call her back, just to be super clear about everything. But no, I know Joy better than that. She understood what I meant. Pressing the issue further will probably make her shut down completely. I can't risk that happening while I'm a million miles away.

"Damn," I sigh, setting my phone aside. "Damn, damn, damn."

I close my eyes and say a silent prayer that my little sister will be okay, then I take a deep breath and try to pull myself together.

Unfortunately, Joy isn't my only concern right now. I need to look after Isla and check on Keir. And, with any luck, I can do all of that while staying as far away from Keir's mother as possible.

I scan the sand dunes and the scrubby hillside in the distance as Isla runs along the beach in front of me. "Don't get too far ahead," I call out. "I'm older and slower than you are, remember? I can't keep up."

The part I'm not saying out loud is that I want to keep her as close to me as possible in case there's even a hint of trouble. We might be on a fancy private beach, but that won't stop a crazy person with a gun. It won't even stop the paparazzi if they think they'll get a good photo.

"Okay, okay," she laughs, coming back to run circles around me instead. "Do you think this is a good spot to build a sand castle? I don't want it to get washed away."

"We should be fine until the tide comes back in," I say, as if I know what I'm talking about. "But if it does get washed away, we'll just come back out here tomorrow and build a newer, bigger one."

"Yeah!" she cheers, plopping down and scooping up handfuls of sand. "You're going to help me, though, right?"

"Of course I will." I sit down next to her and start adding to the growing mound of sand. "Is this going to be the hill where we build the castle?"

"No, silly." She rolls her eyes. "This is one of the towers."

"Oh, right. A tower. I see it now."

Well, at least our castle building skills seem to be evenly matched. As long as she's happy and smiling, I'm more than willing to sit here and help her build hill-shaped towers all day long.

"My dad was sad before we came here," she says, looking up at me with a seriousness that is completely at odds with the way we've been playing on the beach. "Before we came here, I mean. After you left."

God, how is it that kids know how to tear a person's heart out with just a few innocent words? Joy has always been able to do the same thing. It's maddening. Maybe because both girls are old souls trapped in young bodies. Maybe because kids in general have a knack for seeing through adult bullshit and pretense. Maybe Isla and Joy are simply too smart and mature for their own good sometimes.

Whatever the reason, it never fails to make me want to reach out and hug them, to promise that everything is going to be okay and that things aren't as bad as they sometimes seem.

It's hard to make that promise now, though. Just like I couldn't bring myself to make that same promise to Joy when I was talking to her earlier.

I can still give Isla a hug, though. "I think we can all be happy here for a while," I say, meaning it as I pull her in close. "All three of us. And Saffron."

"And Grandma, too?"

Well, I don't want to lie to the kid. I'm not sure that woman knows how to be happy. But it's a bright, sunny day and there's not much harm in being optimistic.

"Sure," I say, nodding. "Your grandmother, too."

From the corner of my eye, I can see someone moving toward us. My pulse instantly quickens even as I recognize who it is.

Just Keir, thank God. Not the killer. Not the paparazzi. Just tall, dark, handsome Keir.

"Looks like your dad is coming down here to check on us," I whisper, smiling as Isla jumps up and starts running toward him.

'Dad! Are you going to build sandcastles with me and Ella? Please, will you?"

He shoots an inquisitive look in my direction. "Maybe I could join the two of you for a little while."

Is he asking permission? From me? Is this his way of checking to make sure we're on good terms again? It's not like I'm going to object in front of Isla, but I guess it's still nice that he's asking.

"I hope you're better at building sand castles than I am," I answer, watching him as he walks over to sit next to me.

Keir sits down, flashing me a little smirk. "I'm trying to be nicer."

"Nicer?" I ask. "That's not exactly a quality I associate with you. Commanding? Dashing? Absolutely unwilling to do things any other way than you've always done them? That sounds more like you."

He straightens his tie, his eyes flashing. "Well, maybe I am tired of being so inflexible."

"You? Be more flexible?" I can't help the laughter that bubbles to the surface. "I don't think it's possible."

52

"You'll just have to see it in action, I guess." Keir looks amused and sits back, playing with his tie.

Lord, he really is sexy. Sexier than anyone should be in the middle of the day.

It's times like this, seeing him laugh and play and being so attentive, that I can't help but think of how nice it would be to stay with him. To have a real, loving relationship that we can both admit to in public. Better yet, to live somewhere together where we don't have to worry about admitting anything to anyone and where every move we make doesn't end up in the tabloids.

That isn't the world we live in, though. That isn't the kind of life he'll ever have. That kind of relationship won't ever be possible with Keir.

I understand that now. Better than I did before, at least.

And that's why I'm guarding my heart even while I'm letting my mind wander and daydream about a life and a love I know I'll never get to fully experience.

CHAPTER EIGHT

KEIR

I'm just finishing a conference call when I see Ella walk by outside the window.

With a goodbye so quick that it's borderline rude, I hang up with the NewsCorp board and shut my laptop. I take off after her.

I'm still not sure where our relationship stands.

With my mother still here and seemingly lurking around every corner, Ella and I have gone back to playing the roles of employer and employee most of the time. But at least she's smiling more and speaking to me again after that outing on the beach with Isla a couple of days ago, so that's a plus.

And I have my new mantra ringing in my head. *Be nice.* I'm not a hundred percent certain how to go about that, but I'm damn well going to try.

"Hey," I call out to her as soon as I'm outside. She's already halfway down the terraced steps toward the private stretch of beach. She looks so damn sexy in her bikini that I can't help but stop in my tracks and stare when she turns to look back over her shoulder at me.

"What?" she prompts after a few awkwardly silent seconds. "Did you need something? Or did you just come out here to scare me half to death and then stare at me for five minutes?"

I snort because, yeah, I definitely got busted for staring. "It wasn't five minutes," I say, breaking into a light jog to quickly close the distance between us. "I was just, uh, going to ask if you wanted some company out here. I didn't realize you were going down to the beach, though."

"Your mother took Stella and Isla shopping," she shrugs. "So I thought I'd take the opportunity to check out the kayaks I saw in the boathouse down by the beach."

She can't possibly think I'm going to sit back and watch while she kayaks into the ocean by herself, but I know better than to say that part out loud. I don't pretend to understand women in general or Ella in particular, but I do know for sure that she doesn't like to be told what to do.

Ironic, since she's still technically an employee of mine.

"Mind if I join you?" I ask, doing my best to avoid sounding overly protective. She can't accuse me of controlling her life if I'm asking for permission, right? "I haven't laid eyes on those kayaks in years. It'll be fun to see if I can still maneuver in one without tipping over."

"You really want to go kayaking?" A small smile spreads across her pretty lips. "With me?"

"I do. Is that okay?"

Her smile grows a little wider. "They're your kayaks. I should probably be asking you."

"They're technically my mother's kayaks," I say with a rueful grin of my own. "As I'm sure she'd be happy to remind us. But I'm not going to bother asking her permission. It's easier to ask forgiveness afterward."

She laughs as we start walking down the steps toward the beach together. "Since when do you ask forgiveness for anything?"

"Good point. We won't ask her anything at all."

Bit by bit, step by step, I can see the walls starting to come down. I can't blame her for putting those walls up in the first place, of course, but it's nice to be around each other without so much tension and animosity between us.

The kayaks are in good shape, just a little dusty. Ella is actually having an easier time with hers than I am as we take them out and start paddling along the rocky coastline.

"It's so beautiful out here," she shouts back over her shoulder. "We should do this more often."

I'm too busy trying to stay upright to pay much attention to the natural beauty all around us. Ella watches me for a moment, a smile on her lips.

"What?" I ask. "Can't a man try to maneuver his kayak in peace?"

She gives me a long, thoughtful look. Finally she shrugs and says, "I see it."

"See what?" I mutter.

I don't remember kayaking being this much of a struggle. It's probably been at least fifteen years, maybe longer, since I've had to balance myself against the gentle but relentless lapping of the ocean waves.

"I can see you trying to be more flexible. I think a few months ago, you would have just stood on the shore and watched as I paddled the kayak. Now you're in the water with me. That's progress."

A grunt leaves my lips. "We don't have to pick it apart."

Ella shrugs a shoulder. "I'm just saying that I have noticed you trying to soften your approach and be less rigid. And I appreciate it."

My first instinct is to snarl at her. But I catch the sound and cut it off before it rises in my chest. Instead, I give her a grudging "thanks."

"No problem." She beams at me. "Now the question is… can you keep up with me? This is a young person's game."

She gives me a mischievous look and splashes me with her paddle. I growl and dig my paddle into the water.

"Bring it on, young blood."

Getting older is a pain in the ass, but I'm not about to admit it out loud. Yeah, this probably wasn't the best idea I've ever had, but I did invite myself, so I only have myself to blame.

At least my muscle memory is finally starting to kick in, and I'm remembering how to time my paddling so I'm not fighting against the current the entire time. I even feel confident enough to look around after the first few tense, shaky minutes have passed.

And of course the first thing I see is a fucking photographer. I feel a surge of anger rising up even as I try to give him the benefit of the doubt. Maybe he's just a tourist. Maybe he's taking pictures of the ocean, the seagulls, or the beach.

Except no, he isn't.

His camera lens is trained on me and Ella. He's even following us, walking along the shore parallel to our kayaks.

"Fucking bastard," I mutter, paddling faster so I can pull up next to Ella.

"Looks like we have some company," she says once I've moved closer. There's irritation and a hint of fear in her tone as she looks from me to the photographer and back again. "How did they find us? I didn't think there would be any paparazzi at all on this tiny island, of all places."

"There normally aren't," I grumble. "That's why I wanted to come here." I point to a rocky outcropping a few hundred yards ahead. "There's a small cove on the other side of those rocks. We can hopefully lose him there, since he'll have to climb over some rough terrain to catch up."

Her brow furrows. "How are we going to lose him there? Isn't a cove sort of like a bay? Aren't we going to be sitting ducks if we go there?"

"Trust me. We'll get him to leave us alone one way or another."

It only takes a few minutes to make it past the outcropping. I exhale a relieved breath when the cove comes into view.

"There," I point, glad my memory hasn't failed me and that not much has changed in the years since I've seen this secluded spot. "See that waterfall? There's a cave behind it. That guy won't know where we are as long as we get there before he shows up."

Ella doesn't need any other prodding. She zips ahead of me and climbs out of her kayak as soon as we make it to the rocky beach. It isn't until we're starting to climb the short distance up to the base of the waterfall that I realize she's wincing more and more with each step.

"Are you okay?" I ask, dropping my kayak so I can wrap an arm around her waist. "Just leave your kayak there with mine. We'll get behind the waterfall faster that way."

"But he'll be able to find us easier if we leave them there." Even as she argues, she follows my lead and drops her kayak next to mine. "Sorry, I didn't think my leg would bother me today."

"You don't need to apologize. Is it the same muscle you pulled when we were being chased at the airport?"

She nods and I can feel myself getting angry all over again. I'm angry with the guy who nearly ran her down and nearly shot both of us that day in Glasgow. Angry with the paparazzi who are forcing us to hide when we should be out there enjoying ourselves on the water. Angry with myself for allowing any of this to happen in the first place.

I promised Ella that she would be safe with me. I'll be damned if I'm going to let her down again.

There's a small, dry alcove behind the waterfall. Not quite

as large as a cave, but more than enough space for the two of us to sit and rest without being seen.

"Sit here on this big rock," I say, easing her down and then crouching in front of her. "I'll massage your leg if you want to prop it up on my lap."

She must really be in pain, because she doesn't even offer a token argument this time. "Don't press too hard, okay?" is the only thing she says as I start gingerly rubbing her calf muscles.

"I won't. I'll take it slowly and gently, just like this." I'm watching her expression for any signs of pain as I move my hands up to her lower thighs. "Doing okay so far? Is this helping at all?"

"A little," she says, nodding. "Thank you. I didn't mean for this to happen, though. I wouldn't have suggested kayaking if I'd known there would be paparazzi."

"I know. And it isn't your fault." I'm still massaging, but now I'm also keenly aware of just how high on her leg I'm touching her. Can't think about that now, though. This isn't about how sexy she is or how badly I'd like to get her out of these clothes and feel her warm body next to mine, bare skin against bare skin. "It feels like no matter where we go, the paparazzi are one step ahead. That's probably something you were looking forward to leaving behind in Glasgow."

"Can't argue with you on that one," she sighs. "I'd like to say I'm getting used to all the non-stop attention that you have to deal with every day of your life, but... I'm not. I don't know if I could ever get used to it."

Now it's my turn to wince. I know she isn't intentionally trying to hurt me, but her words are just one more reminder that we're completely mismatched as a couple. We come from different backgrounds. We're moving in different directions. Am I still clinging to her now out of stubbornness? Because I'm comfortable with her?

No.

Not entirely, anyway.

More than anything, I also want to keep her safe. That reason is bigger and more important than any other leftover feelings I might have for her.

"What would you be doing if you'd gone back to New York like you'd planned?" I ask, curious to know just how different her life might be without me in it. "In an ideal world, I mean. If you could do anything you want."

She doesn't hesitate. "I'd start a dance school for young girls. I'd make sure it was affordable to families of all different backgrounds and financial means."

I stop massaging her leg for a moment so I can study her face while I take her words in. "I can picture that pretty easily. You're great with kids. you wouldn't have made it into the New York Ballet if you weren't a serious, skilled, talented dancer. Seems like it might be a thankless job, though. One where you probably won't earn nearly as much as you deserve."

She shrugs. "It isn't always about the money, Keir. And I'm sure it will be thankless at times, but think about all the times you've seen Isla's face light up when she learns something new or when she tells you about something she's accomplished."

I automatically find myself smiling as my thoughts turn to my daughter. "So not totally thankless," I say, digging a little deeper and looking past my initial doubts. "Seeing that look on a young face would be pretty rewarding all by itself, I'd imagine."

"Exactly. Spending so much time with Isla has only made me more determined to find a way to make my little dance school idea a reality."

The more we talk about it, the more I realize just how

perfectly suited she is to that sort of work. And, as usual, it's another indication of how different we are. My first thoughts instinctively went to profitability, sustainability. longer-term scaling opportunities, but I was totally overlooking her reasons. Her priorities. Her dreams.

"I have faith in you," I say, meaning it. "I know without a doubt that you can and will make it happen."

Her expression softens, and I can't help myself. I gently ease her leg down from my lap, then move up to sit next to her on the large rock. She leans in and makes a tender, contented sound in the back of her throat as our lips meet.

I could live forever and never get tired of the way she tastes or the way her body melts against mine every single time we kiss. She's intoxicating in a way I can't explain or justify. I just know that the more I try to deny my feelings for her, the more desperate I become.

"You make me want to be a better man," I whisper.

"I think you are a great man," is her answer. "Not a perfect man, but great nonetheless."

A flurry of movement and a flash of light from the corner of my eye break the quiet, magical moment and leave me with that familiar feeling of rage bubbling up as I recognize the photographer from earlier.

"You son of a bitch," I growl, standing up and moving to block his view of Ella. "I'm gonna smash your fucking camera against these rocks." I lunge toward him. "Then I'm gonna smash your fucking face."

"Keir!" she calls out after me, but I'm already chasing him as he disappears around the edge of the waterfall. "Keir, stop. Please! It isn't worth it."

My fists are clenched, and I have to make the split-second choice between chasing after him and going back to take care of Ella.

It isn't a choice at all, of course. Not really. The last thing I'm going to do is leave her by herself with an injured leg while I chase down some piece of shit photographer.

Still, that bastard had better hope I don't see him again. He might not get so lucky if we cross paths a second time.

CHAPTER NINE

ELLA

The sound of unfamiliar voices puts me on edge as soon as I make it down the stairs. It's still early enough that I could easily sleep for another couple of hours, but I want a little time to myself before Isla wakes up and the whirlwind of planning her day begins.

I love her as if she were my own little sister. I also love the fact that she and Joy seem to be video-chatting almost every single day, but being a live-in nanny is exhausting at the best of times. I've learned to guard and cherish every minute of quiet solitude I can scrape together.

Which is one of the main reasons why my teeth are clenching at the sound of so many extra voices coming from the kitchen first thing this morning.

The other reason is that every time I've come across a stranger over the past week or so, they've either tried to take my picture or kill me. I'm not exactly in a hurry to find out which category these new people will fall into.

Who are they?

What are they doing?

Why are they even here?

Once I make it to the kitchen door, I stop and lean in,

cocking my head to the side. I'm close enough to make out their individual voices now. I belatedly realize they aren't strangers at all.

Those voices belong to the cook and the butler from Drummond Castle.

Feeling a rush of relief mixed with recognition, I push the door open and slip inside the kitchen with a sleepy smile spreading across my face. My earlier irritation is almost completely forgotten as I look back and forth between the staff members. "Good morning. Good to see both of you," I say, making a beeline for the coffee. "God, I've missed your coffee."

"You don't have to call me God," the cook says with a wink. "We heard things have been a bit hectic lately."

"So here we are," the butler stands up straight and adjusts his waistcoat, his delivery as dry and deadpan as ever, despite the twitching of his lips. "We've arrived to save the day."

"I'm really glad you're both here," I say, pouring my coffee and inhaling the deliciously caffeinated scent. "It's nice to see some familiar, friendly faces."

Before any of us can say another word, a short, angry man in an expensive-looking suit bursts into the kitchen and fixes me with a stern glare. "Why aren't you in the meeting?"

I'm so caught off guard that it takes a moment for my brain to catch up. Even then, I have to look around to double check that he's talking to me. "I, um," I pause to look over at the cook and butler, but they just shrug and take a step back. "What meeting?"

The man's mouth drops open and then closes again with a snap. "Are you seriously that incompetent? Where did Lord Greyrose find you?" He's the one who turns to face the butler this time. "Why can't we ever seem to find a good assistant? Natasha might have been crazy, but at least she came to work prepared to *work*. "Unlike," he huffs out a short breath and makes an impatient motion toward me. "Unlike this one."

Okay.

I don't know who this man is or what in the world he's so upset about, but I'm not going to let him talk to me this way. Especially since I haven't had even a sip of coffee yet.

"Listen," I say as I point at him and take a step in his direction. I'm not normally a very confrontational person, but he's pushed every single one of my buttons this morning. all at the same time. "I don't know where you came from or what you think you're doing in here, but there's only one person in this house I take orders from. His name is—"

"That's me." Keir's deep, booming voice fills the room as he appears behind the angry man, startling him visibly. "She takes orders from me. She's Isla's nanny, not my assistant." He crosses the room to stand next to me, glaring at the flustered little guy the entire time. "She sure as hell isn't your assistant. Do you want to know what it's like to be yelled at in front of your co-workers?" His voice is rising with each word until he is, in fact, yelling. And he doesn't wait for an answer before continuing to lay into the guy. "You don't get to come into *my* house and order *my* staff around. Ever."

"I'm s-sorry, sir," he stammers as the color drains from his face. "I didn't mean to offend. I can see I was out of line."

"Indeed," Keir nods, not giving the man an inch of grace. "You were offensive, and you were out of line, but you don't owe me an apology. I'm not the one you thought you were going to yell at and belittle when you came marching in here, so high and mighty and full of yourself."

This is far from the first time I've witnessed Keir dressing down an employee, but it is the first time I've been silently cheering him on. I'm a firm believer in treating others the way I want to be treated. I always assume most people feel the same way. But when someone starts acting so aggressive and rude for no apparent reason, I don't mind putting them in their place.

Or in this case, seeing someone else put them in their place.

"I'm sorry," the man says for the first time since his outburst. "I was out of line and I shouldn't have spoken to you the way I did. I can assure you it won't happen again."

I nod but don't say anything else. Keir keeps glaring at him until he slowly backs out of the room and disappears.

From the corner of my eye, I see the butler nudging the cook, then silently ushering him out of the kitchen as well. Only now, once Keir and I are finally alone, do I let myself exhale a pent-up breath.

"That was crazy," I shake my head and look over at Keir. "Who was that guy, anyway?"

"It doesn't matter," he says dismissively. "He won't ever bother you again. I'm going to fire him before he leaves today, but I'll let him sweat it out a little more first."

I feel a pang of guilt even though the guy really was acting like a rude, condescending asshole. "You don't have to fire him, do you? He did apologize after you put him in his place."

"He should have offered that apology before I demanded it. Just like he should do the right thing and offer his resignation before I demand it. I doubt that's the course he'll take, though." He shrugs. "Regardless, I have to get rid of him. He's shown who he really is and how he really acts when nobody is around to stop him. That's the kind of negativity that can fester and grow within an organization. God knows that's the last thing NewsCorp needs right now."

I nod because I know he's right. As much as I hate to see someone lose their job, especially when it was partially because of me, I also understand where Keir is coming from as a leader. That guy's actions reflect poorly on himself, on

66

Keir. the entire organization. Those actions obviously can't go unpunished.

"Still doesn't feel good," I say, finishing my thoughts out loud. "But I can't blame you for letting him go. It's the right thing to do."

He opens his arms and pulls me into a half-hug. "It's better than the alternative. I wanted to punch him right in his disrespectful mouth when I heard him talking to you like that, so you should be proud of me that I managed to restrain myself."

A small laugh escapes before I can stop myself. "You? Exercising restraint? I guess I didn't get the weather report about Hell freezing over."

He looks genuinely surprised for a split-second before he snorts and playfully pushes me away. "And here I was feeling bad because he yelled at you. I forgot how well you can hold your own."

"I blame you. I used to be nice and sweet before I started working for you." I can only hold back my own playful smile for a few seconds before adding, "Seriously, though, thank you for sticking up for me. And for what it's worth, I think you have learned to exercise restraint more often. That's the first time in a while that I've seen you go after someone like that. It was totally deserved in this case."

Several long seconds pass while he holds my gaze. Finally, he nods approvingly, with a hint of a smile still visible. "I feel like we're starting to understand each other a little better than we did before. I wish we'd been able to get to this point sooner."

He walks away without saying anything else, leaving me to mull over his words on my own. For the second time in as many minutes, I find myself agreeing with him.

We really do seem to have a better understanding of each

other these days. And yeah, it makes me wish for the same thing—that we'd found a way to get here sooner.

If we had, it might have changed the trajectory of our entire relationship.

"Ella?" Saffron's normally-assertive voice carries a hint of uncertainty that makes me look up from the TV as she walks into the living room. "Do you have a second?"

"Sure," I nod, patting the sofa cushion next to me. "What's going on? Is everything okay?"

She offers a sheepish smile as she sits down and heaves a drawn-out sigh. "Everything is fine. Good, I mean. It's nothing to worry about; I just thought maybe we could catch up a little since I think this is the first time I've seen you alone since we got here." She pauses and cocks her head to the side. "Unless you'd rather have some peace and quiet? Sorry, I didn't even think about that before I came barging in here."

I know she said not to worry, but she's acting so uncharacteristically unsure of herself that I can't help but wonder what she isn't telling me.

"You didn't barge in at all," I reassure her. "After all, we're in the living room. If I really wanted privacy, I would have stayed in my bedroom." I wait a second, then prompt her when she still looks a little conflicted. "So? What's up? I'm already imagining the worst, so go ahead and put me out of my misery, whatever it is."

Finally, she flashes a genuine smile, followed by another heavy sigh. "Promise not to say anything to my brother?"

I only have to hesitate for a moment. While I don't want to keep anything important from Keir, it's definitely not my place to divulge her secrets to him. Or vice versa, for that matter. The last thing I'm going to do is jump in the middle of whatever sibling drama might be brewing between the two of them.

"All right," I say, nodding. "I promise."

"Right. Well." She looks around the room as if to make sure there isn't anyone else standing around who might overhear. "I have to leave the island for the rest of the summer."

I wait to hear if there's more, but she just looks at me expectantly as if she's dropped some kind of bombshell.

"Okay," I say slowly, still trying to grasp the significance of her revelation. "Are you worried about Keir getting angry that you've decided to leave? He doesn't normally keep tabs on you like that, does he?"

The thought of Saffron cowering in fear of her brother's anger flies in the face of everything I know about her. She's strong, smart, and independent. I've only ever seen Keir celebrate those qualities in his sister. He might be annoyed that she's leaving so soon if she promised to spend the summer here, but I can't imagine him actually staying angry about it.

I also can't imagine her caring this much about something so trivial, if I'm being completely honest.

"No," she admits. "I don't think he'd mind so much if I just went back home to Scotland. It's not like he forced me to come here or anything." She nibbles at her bottom lip as a spark of mischief flashes in her eyes. "But I'm not going back home. I'm going to Los Angeles."

She's leaning in close and whispering the last bit so quietly that it takes a moment to register.

"Oh!" I blink, my breath catching in my throat as my brain finally catches up. "*Oh.* I see. And is it safe to assume that you're going back to L.A. in order to see a certain someone? A certain movie producer?"

"Do you think it's a mistake?" she asks, confirming my suspicions without actually answering my question. "Deacon has already warned me that Keir won't like it if we start seeing each other, but I don't care about that. He'll come around eventually. I'm just worried I'm making a mistake by going all the way out there when there's no guarantee it'll work out."

Unlike Saffron, I'm definitely worried about what Keir will say or do when he finds out what's going on. But I also share her concern about traveling so far and risking a confrontation with her brother if it turns out Deacon isn't interested in her.

"Has Deacon said anything else?" I prod. "Do you know how he feels about starting a relationship? Particularly a long-distance relationship?" I've stopped trying to hide the doubts in my tone as I continue. "Please tell me that's something the two of you have discussed before now."

"Well," she winces, doubling my worries in an instant. "He hasn't spelled it out in so many words. I think he still mostly sees me as Keir's younger sister. If I'm there on my own, I know for sure it'll be a different story. There won't be any other distractions. He won't have to worry about my brother scowling at him or threatening him every time he looks at me. It'll just be me and him. I think we have a really good shot at making it work."

I can hear the hope in her voice and see it clearly on her face. As much as I'll hate to see the inevitable squabble between her and Keir, I can't help but share her same hopeful optimism for her relationship with Deacon.

"I won't pretend I'm not surprised," I say. "But I admire what you're doing. Sometimes you have to take a chance on love, and follow your gut and your heart when people try to persuade you otherwise. That's why I'm still here even though..." I clap a hand over my mouth as I realize what I am about to say.

Good lord, did I seriously almost admit my feelings for Keir? Did I tell Saffron, almost casually, that I'm in love with her brother?

I cringe, preparing myself for her shocked reaction.

Except she doesn't seem shocked at all. My own eyes are wide, and my heart is racing, but Saffron is grinning from ear to ear.

"Oh, Ella!" She throws her arms around me and hugs me tightly. "It's about time you admitted the two of you are in love."

"But," I shake my head, still stunned by what I almost said. "That isn't what I meant. I shouldn't have said anything."

My stomach is starting to hurt. While I'm glad she doesn't seem surprised or upset at all, I still don't think I'm ready to talk about my relationship with Keir. Mostly because I'm fairly certain that relationship no longer exists. What we have now is more of a truce. An understanding, like he said earlier.

But not love.

Not the kind of love she's hoping for with Deacon. Not the kind of love that would make my face light up like hers is now.

"Whatever," she sighs, releasing me from the hug but still beaming. "You can keep denying it if you want, but you'll have to do a better job of pretending if you expect anyone to believe you aren't totally, madly in love with him."

Ugh, how am I supposed to respond to that? She won't believe my denials. I hardly believe them myself.

"It doesn't matter how I feel," I shrug, suddenly exhausted and depleted after her emotional roller coaster ride. "It isn't going to happen between me and your brother. But you and Deacon?" Her smile is starting to dim, but it perks right back up again at the mention of Deacon's name. "The two of you have potential. Real potential. I'm glad you're not going to let it pass you by."

"I won't. And you shouldn't, either. "Like I said, you can

deny it all you want, but," she winks as she gets up from the couch and walks toward the kitchen. "I know the truth."

Lord, she's impossible. I wouldn't change anything about her, though. Goodness knows I'm going to miss her when she leaves.

CHAPTER TEN

KEIR

I'm trying to focus on the laptop screen in front of me, but I can feel Ella's presence in the doorway. it's... distracting.

Just like everything else about her. She's beautiful, graceful, and smart. She lights up every room she's in, even when she's standing still. And now I've apparently fallen so far that she can make me lose my entire train of thought without even saying a word.

"Do you need something?" The words come out rougher than I intend as I finally look over at her. Her face falls, and I instantly feel like an asshole, then feel even worse when I see the worried look that's etched on her pretty face. "What's wrong? Do I need to fire someone else today?"

At least that question brings a hint of a smile to her lips. Maybe that'll make up for the rude greeting I just gave her.

"No," she says, shaking her head, then coming to a halt. "Well, maybe? I'm not sure."

I blink. "Okay, you've just given me three different answers to that question. I was mostly joking, but now I'm not sure." I push my chair back from my desk so I can stand up and move closer to her. Even here in the safety of the villa, my first instinct is to be near her, to protect her however I can. "Tell me what's going on. Whatever it is, I'll fix it."

"I'm sorry," she begins. "This is probably going to sound dumb, paranoid, or both." She pauses for a moment before blurting out the words. "I think one of your security guards might be the guy from the airport. The guy who tried to kill us. I know it sounds crazy and maybe I *am* crazy, but I just get this vibe from him. A really bad, scary vibe. And the way he looks at me when you're not around, it's like…"

She chokes on the last word. She is visibly starting to shake.

Jesus.

Whatever the hell is going on, it must be serious for her to be acting this way. Ella might be high-strung sometimes, but she isn't crazy. She isn't prone to dramatics or hysterics just for the hell of it.

"I believe you," I say, unable to stop myself from crossing the last few feet between us and taking her into my arms. I know I've already blurred the lines between employer and employee beyond all recognition, but fuck it. Our relationship is already complicated, so one more hug isn't going to make it worse. I can't just stand here and watch her suffer, though. That's not going to happen as long as I have the power to stop it.

"I believe you, Ella," I repeat, just to make sure she understands that I'm on her side. "I don't think it sounds dumb, crazy, or any of those things. Has this guy done anything to you? Made threats or said anything inappropriate?"

She shakes her head, her whole body still trembling, as I skim my hands up and down her back to comfort her. "No, nothing like that. It was just a weird feeling at first, sort of like a hunch that something wasn't right whenever I would see him." She swallows hard, her eyes welling up with tears.

"But the more I looked at him, the more I started to recognize him. His body type. The way he moves. The way he looks at me, I swear to God those things are burned into my mind, Keir. He's the guy."

My head is spinning, and I don't know what to think. I do believe Ella, without a doubt. She wouldn't be acting this way on a hunch. Even if it turns out that she's mistaken, I'd still rather be safe than sorry.

I just can't figure out why a member of my security team would want to hurt her. Or me, for that matter. What would they stand to gain?

"Let's go," I say, taking her hand and leading her to the door. "I need you to show me who it is."

She freezes in her tracks. "No. I can't, Keir. I don't want to go near him. I-I can't confront him, even with you standing next to me."

"I don't want you to confront him. I don't want you to go anywhere near him, whether I'm with you or not. But I still need you to point him out to me." I plant a quick kiss on her forehead. "That's all I'm asking, I promise. I'll take care of the rest."

At least she seems to relax a little once I make it clear she won't have to speak to the guy. We walk out into the living room together, and it doesn't take long at all to find him. Ella leads me to the large window overlooking the front of the property and subtly points toward the driveway while flattening herself against the wall at the same time.

"There," she whispers, as if he might hear us from all the way in here. "Over there at the end of the driveway. One of the guys guarding the gate."

My stomach clenches as I take a good look at him. He's wearing a black suit and dark, reflective sunglasses that completely hide his eyes. Just like she said, he's about the right height and build to be the biker from the airport. It's more than just his physical traits, though. It's the way he's standing, the way he's looking, and the energy he's giving off.

"I see what you mean," I say, believing her now more than ever. "And I think you're right. I think he's the guy."

She reaches for my arm, clinging to me. "What are you going to do?"

"Go upstairs and call the police," I say, gently pointing her in that direction. "Then go to Isla's room and stay with her until they get here."

"All right," she says, swallowing hard. "But what are *you* going to do?"

"I'm going to have a word with the guy who almost killed us."

"No, Keir," she gasps and tugs at my arm. "Please don't go out there. It isn't worth it. Please."

"I have to see him up close. I need to look into his eyes. I'm not going to make any accusations or try to fight him or anything, I promise. But I have to know for sure."

Thankfully, she doesn't try to argue. She releases my arm and takes off for the stairs, only looking back over her shoulder at me once before disappearing down the hallway to her room.

I take a deep breath and steel my nerves for whatever is about to happen. Like I said, I don't want to confront the guy. He's bigger than I am and clearly has no qualms about trying to kill me, so yeah, I'll let the police worry about trying to take him down when they get here.

I just want to have a conversation with the guy. I want to look into his eyes and see if I still feel the same way about him, if I can still feel that evil energy radiating from him.

Without really knowing what I'll say or do when I'm actually face-to-face with the guy, I walk out of the house and start down the driveway.

This is probably a mistake. It was almost definitely a mistake. There's nothing nonchalant about the way I'm striding across the property or the way I'm keeping my eyes focused on this murderous bastard, but I can't make myself look away.

You tried to kill her.

You tried to kill both of us.

I want to shout those words at the top of my lungs. I want to grab him by the collar and beat the shit out of him. I want to make him feel the same kind of fear and panic that Ella and I felt that day when he was shooting at us and trying to run us down.

He's watching me. I can't see his eyes behind the mirrored sunglasses, but I can still feel him looking at me. Sizing me up. Assessing the situation. Trying to figure out what I'm doing.

There are three other security guards around the perimeter of the estate, but all I can see is the one in front of me. Is he the same guy who killed Max and Wendy?

Maybe I'll ask him once the police come to haul him away.

Hell, maybe I'll ask him now.

"Excuse me," I call out once I'm within earshot. "I need to have a word with you."

So much for a nonchalant, casual tone. I'm just too worked up to fake it, too angry to pretend I don't want to strangle the guy.

I'm about twenty feet away from him now. I'm trying to memorize every detail I can, but my anger is turning to rage with each step I take, until it's like a red mist that's clouding my vision and closing in from all sides.

Just as I open my mouth to say something else, he turns and bolts toward the gate, then scales it and lands on the other side with a thud.

"Hey!" I shout as I start to run after him. "Wait! *Wait*!"

He's already halfway down the block by the time I reach the gates. All I can do is watch him run away as I furiously rattle the metal bars. I gesture for the other guards to follow, but it's pointless now.

He's gone.

CHAPTER ELEVEN

ELLA

How is it possible that Isla can be so much smarter than I was at her age? She truly is an old soul trapped in a kid's body. It only takes about five seconds for her to realize something is wrong when I walk into her bedroom and close the door behind me.

"Have you been crying?" she asks. "Did my dad make you cry?"

Bless her heart. How many times has she heard us arguing? How much does she know, in spite of our best efforts to keep all of the conflict and drama as far away from her as possible?

"No," I say, forcing a smile. "Nothing like that, sweetheart. Your dad and I are getting along great. Really, we are."

At least I'm not lying. Not this time. While it might be a little bit of a stretch to say we're getting along *great*, things have been mostly calm and peaceful between Keir and me while we've been in Malta.

If it weren't for his mom and the paparazzi and the psycho security guard, who almost certainly tried to kill us, things really would be pretty great all around.

"Okay, so what is it?" she inquires, approaching me with a mixture of curiosity and concern on her face. "You're acting funny."

"How am I acting funny?" I keep smiling, avoiding her question with another question as I reach down and give her a hug. "I was just coming in to check on you. Nothing funny about that, is there?"

"But you didn't knock. You always knock before you come in here."

Damn.

Forget being smarter than I was as a child. This kid is smarter than I am right now.

"I wasn't thinking," I say, which is also completely true. "I just wanted to check on you and see what you were up to. Are you hungry? Because I'm starving. Should I have some food brought up here for us?"

Oh God. Now I'm rambling. I really am terrible at lying and pretending nothing is wrong when it feels like my whole world is falling apart.

Or maybe Isla just knows me too well after all this time. Maybe it's because kids only deal with emotions, not logic. She can see right through my babbling and my diversions. But I have to keep this charade going for a little while longer, at least until Keir comes back inside. I'll leave it up to him to reassure me *and* Isla that everything is going to be okay.

A knock on the door behind me makes me jump nearly a foot into the air as a startled squeak escapes the back of my throat. "Who is it?" I demand, scooping Isla up into my arms and moving away from the door as fast as I can.

"It's me," Keir's voice is deep and calm as he opens the door and peeks inside. "Everyone good in here?"

I nod, exhaling as I set Isla back down on her feet. "Why is everyone acting so funny?" She looks from Keir to me and back again. "Tell me!"

If this were any other situation, I'd probably be laughing at her impatience right now. She definitely inherited her father's temper and his imperious attitude, traits that will no doubt serve her well in the cutthroat world she's been born into.

"We aren't acting funny," Keir says, offering the same denial I gave just a few moments ago. "But I do have some exciting news for both of you."

His tone is excited and animated and obviously forced, but it's enough to distract Isla. She might be smart, but she's still a kid. "What exciting news?" she asks, bouncing over to him. "Are we getting a puppy?"

I can't hold in my laughter this time. The sheer look of horror that crosses Keir's face at the thought of a puppy running around the house is comedy gold.

"Not a puppy," he says quickly, shaking his head. "But still something fun. I think we've spent enough time at the ocean, so we're going to the mountains!"

The room is silent after his too-loud, too-enthusiastic statement. I can tell from the scrunched up look on her face that going to the mountains wasn't on Isla's short list of things to do.

"Skiing?" Keir adds, tossing me a pleading look. "And there's a spa…"

I kneel down next to Isla and smile. "We can build a snowman and have hot cocoa by the fire. That'll be fun, right?" I have to admit that I'm warming up to the idea as I continue. "And we'll have snowball fights and make snow angels, too."

"Snowball fights! Snowmen!" Isla cheers. "Yeah! Let's go!"

"Thank you," Keir mouths silently as I stand up and walk over to him. "You saved my butt on that one."

"Glad I could help." I nod toward the door. "What about

the situation downstairs?"

"Everything is fine for now. I'll tell you more later." He leans in closer and drops his voice even lower. "Right now, I need you to help Isla pack her things. then get your stuff packed as well. We're leaving for Switzerland as soon as the police get here."

That's all the information I need.

I trust Keir, and I know he's going to take care of us, but I'll feel a lot safer once we're on the plane and heading as far away from this little island as possible.

I'm reluctant to step off the plane when we touch down in Gstaad, Switzerland, but my hesitation has nothing to do with the freezing cold weather or the strong winter storm heading straight for the resort where we'll be staying.

If anything, I'm looking forward to the change of pace from island getaway to winter wonderland, but I can't pretend I'm not nervous about being among a bunch of strangers again.

Keir has assured me a dozen times already that we'll be perfectly safe with the new security firm he's hired, but I'd honestly rather stay on the plane with Keir and Isla, where I know for sure there are no lunatics hiding in the shadows. The only drawback would be spending more time than necessary in these cramped quarters with Keir's mother, but I'd rather take my chances in the air with her than on the ground with a killer.

At least the sudden need to get out of Malta gave Saffron the excuse she needed to escape to Los Angeles without any unnecessary drama.

"Come on, Ella," Isla says as we prepare to exit the private jet. "Look at all the snow! We can start building a snowman as soon as we get on the ground."

I grin, pushing my worries aside for now. "You want to build a snowman here at the airport? Wouldn't it be better if we waited until we got to the resort? Then we can build a whole snowman family outside the window of your room if you want."

Just as I'd anticipated, her entire face lights up at the prospect of building multiple snowmen. I might be terrible at lying, but I'm getting better and better at bargaining.

Even Keir seems impressed. "Nice move," he says as he leans in from behind me, his deep voice barely above a whisper, and places his hand on the small of my back. "You know the way to her heart, that's for sure."

I turn to look back at him over my shoulder, my smile slipping just a little when I see his mom giving me the stink eye as she follows behind us. "Behave," I murmur as his hand drifts down to my ass. "Don't want to cause a scene." Clearing my throat, I continue, "I might know the way to her heart, but I doubt I'll be feeling so clever when I have to follow through on my promise and make a bunch of snowmen out in the freezing cold."

He laughs. "Good point. I might have to come out and rescue you if it gets too cold." With a smirk, he adds, "Or if my daughter starts getting too demanding."

The icy wind hits my face as soon as we take our first few steps off the plane. I suck in a deep breath to brace myself against the sudden change in temperature. Even Isla looks like she's decided against playing in the snow for now. is running ahead of us as fast as she can toward the waiting SUV.

Gstaad feels like it's an entire world away from Malta even though it's been a relatively short flight, but I guess that's the point. We're supposed to be leaving the worry, the anxiety, and the killer behind us. The police can handle him while we stay as incognito as possible here in the mountains.

But traveling with Keir and his entourage is never a subtle, incognito experience. I just hope we've put enough distance between ourselves and the rogue bodyguard for now. I hope the authorities in Malta will lock him up and throw away the key so he can't hurt anyone else, ever again.

For now, all I can do is trust Keir and try to enjoy the snow-covered resort where we'll be staying.

CHAPTER TWELVE

KEIR

I can't remember the last time I smiled and laughed so much. After all the running, hiding, and near-death experiences, being in Gstaad feels like an actual vacation. It's like some kind of pressure valve in my soul has been released, and I feel happy and carefree for the first time in a long time.

Okay, maybe not completely carefree. That's probably taking it a little too far.

But the tiny Swiss resort town does a good job of making me feel insulated from the rest of the world. I'm content to stay in this safe little cocoon with Ella and Isla, completely off the radar.

"Dad!" Isla calls out from the breakfast table, where she and Ella are finishing their meals, as I walk into the dining room of our suite. "Can you believe Ella hasn't ever been skiing?"

"You've only been once," I remind her, sitting down at the end of the table and skimming the front page of the news-paper that's waiting for me. "But no, I didn't know that. That answers the question of what we'll do this afternoon."

Isla cheers, and Ella shoots me a pleading look. "We don't

have to do that," she says, wide-eyed. "Like, seriously. I don't mind not knowing how to ski."

"It'll be an adventure," I wink, tossing the paper aside and concentrating on these two important people in my life. The news can wait. Business can wait. I have everything I need right here in front of me. Right here at this table. "It'll be an experience, anyway. You might even like it. It's not like you don't have the balance or coordination for skiing."

"What if I fall, though?"

Isla giggles. "Oh, you'll fall. We'll all fall. That's part of the fun!"

I shrug. "She's not wrong. Give it a shot, at least? Might as well make the most of this place while we're here."

Ella sinks back against her chair and nods, her defeated look in stark contrast to Isla's excited cheering. "Fine. I guess we'll go skiing."

"That's the spirit," I say. "Isla will show you the basics, and I'll be there to catch you if you fall."

There's a slight hint of her sunny smile peeking through her cloudy expression. "You promise?"

"I promise. I'll be right there with you."

That's the easiest promise I'll have to make today.

Powdery white snow swirls around us as Ella eyes the slopes in front of us. "I feel like we're really far up the mountain."

"We're on the beginner track," I say, glad my smile is mostly hidden by my scarf and ski mask. "It won't be as bad as you think. Just have fun with it."

"This isn't my idea of fun," she huffs, then pushes off across the slope to join Isla. "You coming, Keir?"

I laugh. "Oh, now you're suddenly feeling brave? Is that a challenge?"

Isla is waving us forward, chanting, "Race, race, race!" but I don't want to push things too far or too fast.

Ella really has been brave by conquering her fear and coming out here to join us on the mountain. The last thing I want is for her to fall or hurt herself and tarnish what will otherwise hopefully be a fun experience.

"Slow and steady," I call out to her, laughing again as Isla shoots me an annoyed scowl. "We can save racing for next time. Let's just concentrate on staying upright for now."

Something hits my arm, and I look down to see the remains of a powdery snowball fall to the ground just before Isla bursts into a fit of giggles. "Got you! If we can't race, we'll just have a snowball fight."

I open my mouth to tell her we should wait to do that, too, but another snowball sails past me from the other direction, landing at Isla's feet and making her crack up all over again.

"Really?" I look over at Ella and shake my head. "You, too?"

"If you can't beat 'em," she shrugs, chucking another snowball in my direction. "I might as well join 'em."

"I see how it is," I crouch down to pick up some snow, then get pelted from both directions as Ella and Isla close in on me. "You're both going to be in big trouble once we get back to the hotel. You realize that, right?"

Isla sticks her tongue out and tosses another snowball, looking impish and adorable all at the same time. "You'll have to catch us first," she taunts, skiing around me and easily dodging the first snowball I toss in her direction.

Ella's next toss hits me square in the chest, her laughter mingling with Isla's and echoing down the slope of the mountain. "We should have skipped skiing and just started the snowball fight back down there," she says, pointing in the direction of the resort. "At least we would have been closer to the heater. And the room service."

"That's not a bad idea," I say, clutching my arm where Isla has just pelted me again. "I'm going to be covered in bruises by the time we make it back down there at this rate."

Ella looks over at Isla and grins. "Shall we call a truce until we get back to the hotel?"

"*Only* until we get back," she agrees. "But then you'd both better run!" Her infectious laughter spills out again as she gathers up one more snowball and tosses it at me for good measure. "The truce can start now."

I can only shake my head as Isla and Ella start skiing back to the lift together. God help me if the two of them really team up on me. They're the only two people in the world who can melt my heart with a single, simple look.

I wouldn't change a thing about either of them, though. The three of us work well together. We understand each other. And while I know Isla will always be the most important part of my life, it's really nice having Ella here with us.

It wouldn't feel right without her.

A short ski lesson.

A not-so-short snowball fight.

A well-earned lunch and a long nap with the three of us sprawled out on the enormous, overstuffed couch in our suite.

Those have been the high points of the day for me so far. No, not just the day. Those have been the high points of my month, now that I'm thinking about them.

Watching Isla and Ella play together, even if it meant enduring a barrage of snowballs, has been one of the simplest, happiest times I can remember. For all the money I have and all the nice things that money can buy, it's the free stuff that means the most.

Laughter.

Fun.

Love.

It's taken me a long time to understand that those are the most important things in life, but I don't know if I've fully been able to appreciate those things until right now, right here.

Jesus, my family would probably disown me if they knew I was thinking such sappy, mushy thoughts. My parents and my brother are cynical, selfish, and devious. I've been all of those things at various times in my life as well.

But what's the point in having it all if you can't ever enjoy it? What's the point in clawing my way to the top if I can't look out and enjoy the view with the people I love the most?

"What are you thinking about?" Ella whispers. Isla is sleeping between us, exhausted from playing in the snow all day.

I wish more than anything that I could stay right here in this moment with the two of them forever. No cares. No worries. Just the three of us staying safe, warm, and happy.

"Just thinking about how nice it is here," I say, which is mostly true. Ella and I need to have a serious talk about our future, if there's even going to be one for the two of us. But not here. Not now. "And thinking about what we can do tonight. Me and you."

She raises a brow and points at Isla. "I don't think we can do that while your daughter is sleeping on the couch."

I barely catch myself before I burst out laughing. "I'm not talking about doing *that*, though it's not a bad idea for later."

Now she raises both eyebrows. "Okay, so if we aren't talking about sex, what did you have in mind?"

"Maybe it should be a surprise." I gently nudge Isla to wake her. "Let's figure out the babysitting situation, and then you and I can have some grown-up time."

I don't know what my mother has planned for the evening, but I'm hoping she won't protest too much about keeping an eye on her only granddaughter. Even if she does protest, I'll just bribe her.

It wouldn't be the first time. It probably won't be the last.

"Should I start getting dressed?" Ella asks. "And are you going to tell me what I should wear to this surprise event? Is it casual? Dressy? Business?"

This time, I don't try to stop myself from laughing. "Definitely not for business. This trip is all about resting and relaxing. And maybe some dancing."

"Dancing?" She sits up straight on the sofa. "Really? Tonight? You and me?"

"You and me," I say, nodding. "There's apparently some kind of salsa class going on downstairs this evening. It's not a nightclub or anything, but I think it might be—"

"It'll be great," she interrupts, clapping a hand over her mouth when Isla shoots her a sleepy scowl. "Sorry," she says, giving my daughter a half-hug before returning her attention to me. "But yes, it'll be great. I'll be ready in an hour."

I look down at Isla and shrug. "I guess that means you're off to have fun with grandma in an hour."

Isla yawns and stretches like a cat, then sighs. "Do you think Grandma will let me play in the snow?"

"No," I answer truthfully, even though I know it's not what she wants to hear. "But if you behave tonight, I'll take you out to play in the snow first thing in the morning."

"Okay! I'll be good!"

She runs off, and now I'm sitting on the couch by myself, already dreading the promise I just made. It'll be worth it for some alone time with Ella tonight, though.

It isn't often that I willingly volunteer to do something I'm not great at. Especially when it's something I have to do in front of other people.

Salsa dancing class is definitely one of those things that I would never, ever sign up for under normal circumstances.

But being here with Ella somehow makes it bearable. Enjoyable, even.

Mostly because it isn't about me. This is her night, and she's clearly in her element. While it obviously isn't the same as ballet, I can tell that being here and moving around the dance floor scratches an itch that Ella has probably had for a while.

She's smiling and laughing as we shimmy and sway around the room. She's mercifully overlooking my two left feet along the way.

"Thank you for tonight," she says as the class starts winding down. "I didn't realize how badly I needed something like this."

"Thank you for coming here with me," I say, leaning in and planting a light, chaste kiss on her cheek. "I'm glad you had a good time. You deserve it after everything you've done for me."

We keep dancing for a few more minutes before they cut the music off. It's taken until the end of the class for me to feel comfortable with the rhythm and the steps, but now I can finally start to enjoy the beautiful woman in my arms.

She's beaming, radiant, and gorgeous. And I'm the luckiest bastard in the world to be here with her right now. I could honestly keep dancing with her all night if they'd let us. That realization makes me wonder what I'm doing with my life if I'm not making plans for the future with Ella.

She's perfect. Perfect for me, at least. We balance each other out in a way I've never experienced with anyone else before. I doubt I'll ever have it with anyone else again.

I love her.

Ella is the person I think about all day, every day. She's the person I want to be with. The person I want to make memories with.

I just have to figure out how to make it work, how to

overcome our differences and the forces that want to tear us apart. I also have to keep her safe, since there's still at least one person out there who wants to see us both dead.

I don't have to figure any of those things out tonight, though. Tonight, I just have to be in the moment, in *this* moment, with my perfect, sweet Ella.

CHAPTER THIRTEEN

ELLA

"Keir!"

Ella yelps as I pick her up and carry her the last few steps through the snowy terrain to the hotel. We are coming back from a late night stroll, still wearing our warmest winter coats, gloves, and heavy boots. I carry her through the door. She writhes, so I sling her over my shoulder.

"Put me down!" she shrieks. "Keir, seriously..."

"Shhh. Just a minute."

I look around the lobby, trying to decide where to go. There are a few guests still at the hotel's fancy bar and a couple walking toward a hidden bank of elevators. I swivel my gaze to the big oak check in desk, then I see it. A dark little alcove, the corners of the inside of the cubby all but obscured by shadow.

"Ella... you're going to have to trust me for a minute here." I start moving toward it, knowing just what I want to do in that alcove. Mental images of me ripping off Ella's thick wool jacket and unbuttoning her dark jeans immediately bubble to the surface.

Her muffled voice floats up to me from where her face is pressed into my thick coat. "Keir, can you put me down?"

I cross the white shag rug that is spread across the lobby floor, avoiding the curious gaze of the front desk attendant. In a dozen quick paces, I make it just beyond the attendant's view. Stepping into the alcove, I set Ella on her feet.

But instead of moving back, I skim her thighs, catching her dress and tugging it up, leaving her exposed.

"Keir!" she hisses. "Stop it!"

"You don't want that." I kiss her lips, playing with her skin tone panties. "I promise if you let me do what I want, you'll enjoy it…"

Indecision is written all over Ella's face. I palm one of her breasts through the material of her dress. Her nipple emerges through the flimsy material and when I tweak it, her breath hitches.

"Are you sure no one will see us?"

I trail my hand down to her thighs, teasing the sensitive skin I find there. "A better question to ask is, who cares if we get caught? The danger is part of the fun."

I tease the dark triangle of silk that covers her pussy. It dampens under my touch and I know, in that moment, that I'm about to win.

As she sighs, she pulls me down so that I press the length of my body against hers. "Keir... oh god, Keir..."

The way she says my name makes me *wild*.

My cock gets as stiff as steel as I press it into the heat of her silky thighs. I snarl and kiss her behind the neck, sucking at the tender flesh I find there. "I can't wait to fuck you like you've never been fucked before, sweetheart."

She blinks her eyes open and pins me down. "Please take me, Keir," he pleads. "God, please fuck me. Touch my pussy. Make me come."

Yes, yes, and yes. I rip her dress down her arms and bunch the bottom up around her waist. I need her right now, nothing else will do. *Fuck, she's perfect.*

She takes a big breath and stares me in the eyes as she pulls down her dark strapless bra. "I need you, baby."

I give her a smirk. "Ella... you only have to ask."

She teases her own nipple, making heavy eye contact with me. Her lips part in a breathy moan. "This is me, asking."

I growl. "You know how to get my attention, sweetheart."

She raises her head and kisses me on the lips. I love watching her when she turns into this seductive creature. All that bare skin in front of my eager eyes is almost more than I can handle.

God, she knows just how to turn me on.

As I bend her back, I bite my bottom lip. I slide my hand between our bodies once more and touch the front of the dainty silk triangle. The silk is damp to the touch and clings against her body. Her pussy is wet and ready for me.

I'm salivating, in desperate need of what only Ella has to give me.

Ella raises her head to observe as I lower my lips to her tits. "I've been fantasizing about these for a while. Dreaming about how they taste and feel against my tongue."

I pinch and squeeze Ella's nipple as I begin to nibble on one.

"What are you going to do to me?" she asks, her voice sultry, her eyes showing excitement and anticipation.

I kiss one of her nipples before nipping at her breast, leaving just a whisper of pain. She reacts, squirming and moaning, I make a fist with my cock and rub it against her pussy. I'm so horny for her that a little white fluid leaks from the tip. I brush my fingers over the tip, catching a little of the fluid.

She's watching my hand, her keen eyes on my cock. She leans forward and grabs my fingers, bringing them to her lips and sucking them into her hot, wet mouth.

Fuck. My eyelids flutter closed for a second and my brain

goes into a temporary meltdown. She licks my fingertips clean, sucking on them until the precum is gone.

She slays me. I open my eyes, my body begging for more of her touch.

"Fuck, Ella. See what you do to me? You're so damn hot."

"Please," she begs. "Keir, please. Touch my pussy. Lick my nipples. My body needs you, baby."

I brush a butterfly kiss against her lips. Then I kiss the elegant column of her neck, her collarbone, her magnificent breasts, her flat stomach. She arches her back and moans. I continue to descend, and I use my hand to open her thighs.

"I can't wait to fuck taste you, sweetheart," I say, watching her face. She runs her hands through my hair as I nuzzle my way between her thighs.

I finally get to her pussy lips, which have been dampened by her excitement. Ella's breathing hitches and she presses my face against her pussy.

I'm only too ready to give her exactly what she wants.

I give her a light kiss on the clit. She lets out a loud groan, spreads her legs wide, and presses herself to my mouth.

She requires my assistance. She requires my pleasure, which only I can provide.

I kiss her again, this time deeper, with just a flick of my tongue. Her clit is swollen and plump, ready to be sucked.

But not just yet. I need to torture her some more first.

My tongue runs up the inside of her thigh. She moans and raises her hips. Ella pants my name when I get too close to her clit, but I mercilessly tease her. Instead of the kisses and licks she clearly craves, I blow across her clit.

The answer is yes. "You're killing me, Keir."

"Open your legs wider for me, sweetheart. Maybe I'll stop teasing you."

She moans as she braces her legs wide. Her excitement is

evident, her pussy dripping wet. I test her with a finger, which she pushes against greedily.

I taste her clit and feel her muscles tighten around my knuckle as my finger sinks into her wet pussy. I pull my finger out, despite her best efforts to press against my hand and keep me inside.

"Perfection," I say as I show her the wetness I've spread on my fingertips. "Ella, you're incredibly sweet. Like tasting candy. I'm pretty sure that I could subsist on eating your pussy alone for months…"

Her hips flex as she strains to get her pussy closer to my mouth again.

"Keir!" she cries.

I tease her opening with two fingers while kissing her clit.

"Keir… Lick my pussy," she pleads. "God, your tongue feels so good."

I slide two fingers into her and am rewarded with a needy sound from her lips. I start licking and sucking her clit.

"Oh… oh," she moans. "Yes, fuck yes!"

Ella works her hips against me, seeking fulfillment. I match her rhythm with my mouth. Her innermost muscles start trembling.

When I see her climax approaching, I slow down. I raise my head, run my thumb over her clit, and watch Ella.

God, she's stunning. She is a vision with her head thrown back, eyes closed, and fingers buried in my hair.

"Do you want me to make you come?" I ask.

"Yes!" she shouts, begging. "Keir, please!"

Ella opens her eyes and looks at me through eyes gone dark with lust.

My tongue returns to her clit. I slide my fingers back inside her pussy and she makes a hungry sound. From her opening to her wet clit, I trail my tongue back and forth. Then

I focus on her clit, setting an intense rhythm, flicking my tongue back and forth with vigor.

She digs her fingers into my hair and presses my lips against her clit, hissing. "That's it. That's it…"

I just hang on for the ride, my tongue working furiously to keeping up with the pace she needs. Her hips rock, her breath comes in pants. She fucks my face, my mouth, like it is all she'd ever wanted. Every time she cries out my name, it makes me want her even more.

"Oh fuck… oh fuck…" she yells. She lets out an animal-istic sound from somewhere deep within her. Her eyes roll up in her head as she clenches and spasms.

As she comes, I lick up every last drop of her sweet, sticky wetness. When I kiss her clit one last time, she shivers.

She looks down my body as I rise from my knees. "You're still hard," she says, as if that is a coincidence.

I grin. "Not for long. I'm going to fuck you like you've never been fuck right now."

She wriggles for a split second. She caresses my cock with her hand, but I catch her wrist. She looks up at me, piercing me with her gaze.

"Now it's my turn," I say. "Can you handle my big dick, sweetheart?"

The answer is yes. I know she can; it's as if Ella was built for me.

Her sultry whisper still excites me. "There's only one way to find out, Keir."

I slide into her with ease, positioning myself between her legs, and exhale at how fucking good she feels. Tight, wet, and hot as a furnace.

"Fuck, darling. You're perfect." I can barely get the words out as I hammer my cock into her pussy. Her body grips me and she wraps her legs around me, desperate to make me come. I can see the fire in her eyes.

Ella digs her nails into my lower back to keep me in her embrace.

I begin to fuck her slowly and deliberately, while kissing and sucking at her neck. At the same time, I rub her clit again with my hand.

Her pussy is so hot, and it grips my cock so perfectly. I'm not used to coming quickly. But watching Ella come so hard earlier had an effect on me.

"Ella," I whisper. "Fuck, I'm already almost there."

"Come in me," she groans, her eyes flickering with a dark hungry. "Please fill me up."

It doesn't take much more encouragement. I jackhammer my cock into her pussy. I cry out as the orgasm hits my body like a tidal wave. "Fuck! So... goddamned... good.."

As soon as I come back to earth, I hear a throat clear behind me. Reaching for my pants, I fumble with the zipper as I glance over my shoulder. There is a uniformed desk clerk standing there, glaring at us.

"This is a public place," the clerk scolds. "Please, do your business upstairs, *ja*?"

Ella ducks her head against my chest and scrabbles to pull her dress down. I give her space for a moment, acting as a shield.

"I'll give you a thousand euros to turn around and go on with your night as if you hadn't seen anything." I brandish the money clip in my pocket.

The desk clerk flushes, looking angry, and pulls herself up. "I'll be back in two minutes. You had better be gone."

Ella pulls her coat on and completely covers herself. She's angry, I can tell.

"Keir…" she hisses as soon as the clerk is gone. "You got us caught!"

I wave a dismissive hand. "Like this is the first time she's ever chased off amorous guests."

"Oh, you are just... so damned spoiled." She pushes pasts me, looking both ways before making break to the bank of elevators. She presses the button, fuming.

I follow her, smirking and straightening my shirt. "That's not very nice."

The elevator door opens and Ella slips in, mumbling under her breath. I follow her in, putting my arm around her. At first Ella's body is stiff. But once the doors close, she relents and allows me to drop a kiss in her hair.

CHAPTER FOURTEEN

KEIR

We've been in Gstaad for a little over a week, and I'm starting to chafe at the feeling of being confined in the tiny town. No amount of skiing, dancing, or fucking can make up for the ability to come and go and live my life as I please without looking over my shoulder every five minutes.

Today I even jumped at the chance to take Ella shopping, just so I'd have something to occupy my time.

"What do you think of this one?" she asks, stepping out of the fitting room to model a knee-length pink dress. "Too girly?"

I laugh. "It's a dress. Isn't it supposed to be girly?"

She rolls her eyes. "You know what I mean."

"I have no idea what you mean, unfortunately."

"Is it too pink? Too long? Too short? Too puffy at the waist where it flares out?"

I blink, then shrug. "I like it. You look beautiful in it. Does that help?"

"No," she says as she examines herself in the mirror, then smiles sympathetically at me. "But thank you. I know this isn't what you'd planned on doing this afternoon, but I was seriously out of clothes to wear."

"I didn't have any plans at all this afternoon. That's part of the problem."

She stops on her way back into the fitting room, then turns and frowns. "Problem? What do you mean? Are you getting tired of Gstaad already?"

I have to smirk because she knows me too well. "Honestly? Yes. I like being here with you and Isla, but I hate feeling like we're hiding, like we're fugitives, when the actual criminal is out there running free."

This isn't really the time or place to have a serious conversation about our safety or our living situation, but what do I care if a few Swiss shop clerks hear us?

"I'm surprised you've lasted this long without holding a meeting or doing whatever it is you do at work," she says, finally stepping back into the fitting room but leaving the door propped open just enough for us to continue talking. "Good to know the company can carry on for a week without you, though," she says. "Maybe you'll be able to take some time off more often now that you know everything won't fall apart when you leave the office."

"I still don't know that for sure," I grumble, but it's hard to concentrate or be too annoyed when I have a perfect view of Ella while she changes clothes. Her body is exquisite. I'll never get tired of looking at her. "I like that outfit best," I say when she's down to just her panties and bra.

"You're impossible," she laughs, slipping on another dress as she casts a self-conscious look in my direction. "But I appreciate the compliment."

"If we had a little more privacy, I'd give you more than just compliments," I say, dropping my voice low enough so she's the only one who can hear me. "Another reason why we need to get out of this little town."

"I'm not sure that reason really counts. But anyway, where do you want to go from here? Back to Scotland?"

That's the question I've been wrestling with in my head for the past couple of days. I still haven't made a decision, though.

"What about going back to Malta?" I ask, anticipating her reaction even before I see the frown spread across her face. "Hear me out, okay? We'll have completely new security. Twice as much as before. I've also looked into renting the villa next door to give us even more privacy and twice as much beach access."

"Will we really be safe there? All of us?"

"I don't want to keep running forever. The authorities have assured me that the guy must have left the island and that they'll arrest him the moment he tries to show his face again. I really don't think we'll have to deal with him anymore while we're there. So I think we'll be just as safe at the villa as we are anywhere else, plus we'll have more room to move around. I can also work better from there, since I have my office at the house set up with secure lines."

There are other reasons I'm not mentioning, like the fact that my mother is pressuring me to go back so she can have a social life again. It's not normally something I care about, but I'll do just about anything to avoid having her on my back all day, every day.

Then there's Isla. As much as she enjoys playing in the snow, she also likes being out in the sun and the water. I know she misses having her own bedroom with her own toys to play with.

"It sounds like you've already made your decision," Ella says, changing again to put on the clothes she arrived in. "If that's really what you think is best, I won't try to talk you out of it."

While I'm glad this conversation hasn't turned into an argument, she hasn't exactly given her approval of my plan to go back to Malta.

I stand up and walk over to the fitting room door, then pick up the handful of dresses she picked out to try on. "I don't want you to be upset," I say. "Or to feel unsafe or worried while we're there. I swear, I wouldn't even think of going back, let alone taking you and Isla with me, if I didn't think we'd be safe at the villa."

She nods and reaches for the dresses. "I need to decide which one I want to buy."

She still isn't giving me much input on the Malta situation, but her silence says plenty. Still, I think it's the right thing to do for now.

Speaking of proper things, I take the dress she's holding from her grasp.

"I'm not going to let you pay for these," I say, dodging her attempts to take the dresses from me while I beckon a saleswoman over to help us. "This is the very least I can do for you after you've upended your whole life for me."

"I don't need you to pay for those things, Keir," she says sarcastically. "I didn't come here to spend your money."

I hand off the small pile of clothing to the clerk and turn to face Ella. "Are you angry with me?"

She looks up at me and cocks her head to the side. "No, I'm just worried. It's hard to know what the right decision is —about Malta, I mean. And you're getting on my nerves with this insistence about paying."

"I could say the same," I say, pressing a quick kiss to her forehead when her mouth drops open in predictable shock and outrage. "Let me do this for you, Ella. I hardly ever get to spoil you. You definitely deserve to be spoiled."

"I just don't want you to think that's why I'm with you. Your money is the last thing on my mind. Honestly."

I grab one more kiss, just because I can't help myself. "I know. That's why it's fun for me to spoil you when I get a chance."

We finish at the clothing store and walk out into the chilly midday air again. "This way," I say, pointing to the shop next door. "Let's look around in here for a second. There's something else I'm thinking of getting."

Once we're inside, she stops and gives me a suspicious look. "A jewelry store? The only jewelry you wear is already around your neck."

I reach up, absently feeling the gold chain beneath my shirt. There are two wedding rings dangling from that chain, two reminders of why I shouldn't ever open my heart to anyone again.

Shouldn't.

Since when has that word ever stopped me?

"Maybe I'm going to start wearing more jewelry," I say, shrugging as we walk over to a display cabinet filled with sparkling bracelets. "Or maybe I'm looking to buy for someone else."

It only takes a moment to pick out a diamond and ruby bracelet that I know will look great on her. "Give me your hand," I say, ignoring her stern look as the salesman holds the bracelet open, ready to fasten the clasp around her wrist. "Come on, just try it on. Please?"

She's moving so slowly that I wonder if she's going to jerk her hand away at the last second, but she finally allows him to put the bracelet on her, then takes a moment to rotate her wrist, letting the sunlight catch all the faceted stones.

"It's beautiful," she whispers. "But I can't. Seriously, Keir, it's too much."

"We'll take it," I say over her objections. "I'll pay for it now, and she can wear it out of here, if that's okay?"

I know it's perfectly okay even before the man nods enthusiastically. "Yes, sir. I'll get the payment taken care of right away, sir."

I turn back to Ella while the clerk takes my card. "Please

don't be upset with me. Like I said before, you deserve it. You deserve nice things. Beautiful things for a beautiful woman."

"I'm not upset, Keir." She forces a smile and I know she's lying. She might not be angry, but she's definitely upset. "Thank you for this. For all of this. I don't know what else to say."

"That's all you need to say." Now I'm second-guessing myself. Sure, I pressured her to accept these gifts, but they're *gifts*. Is she really going to be upset with me over a few small presents?

Or maybe she's still upset over the Malta situation. This is just the icing on the cake. I don't fucking know. If it was anyone else, I wouldn't fucking care.

But she isn't someone else.

She's Ella. *My* Ella.

And I do care.

CHAPTER FIFTEEN

ELLA

By the time we've been back in Malta for a full twenty-four hours, it's almost like we never left. The sun is still shining, and the sounds and smells of the ocean are still all around us whenever we step outside. It's hard to imagine there was a killer staying here with us before, but there was.

I remember all too well. My mind keeps wandering back to him whenever I'm by myself and it's quiet in the house.

So I've been doing my best to stay busy and keep moving, which isn't hard to manage in this household. Thank goodness for Isla, though. She really is a godsend. She's happy to keep me company all day, every day.

We're sitting on her bedroom floor, and I'm braiding her hair when she turns her head to look up at me. "Why is your hair different from mine?"

I smile and reposition her to face ahead as I carefully try to figure out how I'm going to reply. "There are lots of reasons why someone's hair might be different from someone else's," I begin. "Some people prefer shorter hair. Some like to keep their hair longer. Some people have wavy hair, and some people straighten out their curls."

"But your hair looks different from mine. It's pretty, but it feels totally different from mine."

"Your hair is just as pretty," I assure her, though I can't help but keep smiling at the sweet compliment. "The way your hair looks and feels also depends on where your ancestors came from. Your ancestors are from Scotland and England, but mine are from a different part of the world. From Africa."

It's a huge oversimplification, of course, but I hope it's enough to satisfy her curiosity for now. I'm qualified to do a lot of things, but teaching genetics is a little outside my wheelhouse.

"Is that why your skin is a different color than mine?" Isla asks, because, of course, my explanation has only sparked more questions in her curious little mind. "Because we have different ancestors?"

"That's part of the reason," I say, nodding. "There are a lot of different factors, but most of the people I'm descended from have darker skin tones and hair that's a similar color and texture to mine. Most of the people you're descended from have lighter skin and lighter hair."

"My dad doesn't have lighter hair," she counters, immediately poking a hole in my theory of evolution.

"True. But your grandmother does. And your mom. So when you have kids, they'll have some of your traits, some of your husband's. Some from people you're descended from."

"That's cool! I can't wait to have kids of my own someday."

"Someday in the distant future," I laugh. "There'll be plenty of time to think about marriage and kids and all that stuff when you're a grownup."

God knows I still spend plenty of time thinking about those things now.

"Are you mad at my dad?" she asks, startling me with the quick change of topic.

"What makes you ask that?" I try to keep my tone casual even though I'm automatically starting to feel defensive. "Did he say I was mad at him?"

"No, but he's been quiet since we've been back here. You've been quiet, too. So that usually means you're mad at each other."

My stomach clenches, but I try to keep braiding her hair like nothing is wrong. I love how smart she is and hate how perceptive she can be at the same time. Kids shouldn't have to worry about whether the adults around them are getting along.

"We're not mad, sweetheart. It's just," I pause, unsure of how much I should say. I don't want to overstep my boundaries, but I also don't want her to have anxiety about my relationship with her dad. "Your father is a very important man. There are some people out there who don't like seeing him spend time with me."

"Those people should mind their own business," she says, making me laugh in spite of the heavy topic.

"I agree, sweetie. But people are always going to have opinions about everything important people do. That's just part of life, so we have to deal with it the best way we can. Your dad and I are still figuring out how to deal with it, but that doesn't mean we're upset with each other."

She's quiet for a few seconds, then looks up at me again. "I like seeing you with my dad. I think you'd be a good girlfriend for him."

I don't know what to say. What *can* I say?

Instead, I keep my mouth shut and pull her in for a big hug. "I can't say what the future holds for me and your dad," I tell her, being as honest as I can while keeping the conversation from swerving too far into personal, adult territory. "But

I promise you'll always be able to talk to me. No matter where you or I happen to be in the world, I'll always just be a phone call, text message, or video chat away, okay?"

"All right," she says, smiling again.

Lord, I've said it before, but this kid is too smart for her own good. And I adore her with every bit of my heart.

My conversation with Isla has been weighing on my mind since this afternoon. I don't want to bother Keir when he already has so much on his plate, but I feel like he needs to know about some of the questions his daughter is asking.

I've been waiting on pins and needles for him to take a break from his meetings. Now he's finally stepped outside onto the patio with a cup of tea.

This is my chance to talk to him, but the ball of nerves in my stomach is growing larger with each step I take.

Will he be upset?

Will he think I've been oversharing details about our relationship with his daughter?

I open the patio door and start talking before I can change my mind. "Keir? Do you have a minute?"

"Always," he smiles, making the ball of nerves grow twice as big. He has no idea. That makes it even harder. "What's up? Come have a seat. Did you want some tea? I can call for another cup."

"No, thank you," I force a smile of my own and take a deep breath as I sit down at the patio table. "I just want to, um, talk about Isla."

His smile fades. "What about Isla? Is something wrong?"

"No, no," I place a hand on his arm, feeling how tense he's suddenly become. "She's perfect. And smart. And growing up so, so quickly." Another deep breath. Then another. "It's just that I think she sees and hears more than we realize. She was asking about me and you today. Whether we're angry at each other."

"She's more mature than I give her credit for. Much more mature than I was at that age." A crease appears between his eyebrows as he speaks. "Why would she think we're upset with each other, though? I'm not upset. Are you?"

"No. That's what I told her. She also stated that she believes I would make an excellent girlfriend for you."

His eyes go wide as he stares down into his teacup. "I see. How did you reply to that?"

He seems to be taking this pretty well, to his credit. Better than I would have imagined. Better than all the worst-case scenarios I've been playing and replaying in my head all afternoon.

So that's a plus, right?

I'm just not sure I can navigate this next part without causing a fight.

"I tried to explain that it's complicated," I say. "That you're an important man and there are people who would be unhappy if you and I were in a relationship." I smirk to myself as I remember the conversation and the look on her precious little face. "She said those people should mind their own business."

Keir bursts out laughing. "That's my girl. Jesus, she's going to be a handful, isn't she?"

"She already is," I agree, relieved that we aren't shouting instead. "But my point in bringing this up is that... we need to figure this out. This situation. *Us.*"

He nods, his expression turning serious again. "Yes, we do. But do we have to figure it out tonight? Right now?"

"No, not right this minute. I don't think either of us is prepared for that conversation right now. But she isn't going to stop asking questions, Keir. And I don't want to lie or keep giving evasive answers. At some point soon, we'll have to decide what we're going to do. This uncertainty isn't good for any of us. I think you know that."

Again, he nods and studies his mostly-empty teacup, letting the silence stretch out between us for what feels like an eternity even though it's probably only been a few seconds.

"I know," he says, finally. His voice is quiet, barely above a whisper. full of emotion when he looks up to meet my gaze again. "And I want to do the right thing, Ella, for both of us. Whatever that happens to be."

He sets the teacup aside and stands up, reaching for my hand and pulling me up with him as well until I'm in his arms. From here, the rest of the world is slowly being drowned out by the sound of his heart beating next to mine. I would happily stay just like this with him until the end of time. If it was just the two of us, if Keir wasn't a father and a public figure, things would be so much simpler. We'd be together, and we'd be able to tell anyone who didn't like it to fuck off.

That isn't the world we live in, though. That won't ever be our reality. Our reality is this: We have to make the best of our situation. I'm not sure either of us knows what that will look like when it's all said and done.

But I know what I want. I know what my heart wants.

"We'll have that conversation soon," he whispers into my ear as his hands skim down my back. "I promise. Can we keep things simple for now, though? Until the police catch the killer, and we can go back to some version of a normal life?"

"Yeah, we can do that." I'm not sure it's the answer I was looking for, but it isn't as bad as it could have been.

I guess that'll have to be good enough for now.

CHAPTER SIXTEEN

KEIR

I haven't been down to the beach since Ella and I went kayaking a few weeks ago, but I can see her and Isla playing in the sand from my office window, and I want to join them.

It has nothing to do with the fact that I can also see one of our neighbors from the villa down the road out there talking to Ella. Nothing at all to do with that.

He's older than I am and not nearly as rich, though he's probably got close to a billion, if we're keeping track. So it's not like I'm *threatened* by him.

Besides, Ella can talk to whomever she wants, even if that person happens to be an obnoxious loudmouth with more money than taste.

I grunt to myself on my way down the terraced steps to the beach because it occurs to me that people probably say the same thing when they see Ella talking to me.

"How's it going?" I ask when I'm within earshot. My voice is probably a little too loud and definitely a little too sharp. "Hope I'm not missing anything good."

Ella looks surprised to see me. Our neighbor, Louis, looks annoyed. His irritation grows when she takes a small, subtle step to stand next to me instead of him.

And this is just one of the many reasons why I love her.

I hesitate. Did I just have that thought? Do I really love Ella?

As soon as I wonder that, a tsunami of emotion hurls itself down on me. Anguish, loss, fear... But under all that, there is love. A profound amount of love.

God, I'm in love with Ella. The very thought of it is dizzying. I reach out to steady myself as I look at Ella, swallowing hard.

Just what in the hell am I supposed to do with that information?

The real world pulls me from my thoughts in the next second.

Louis cuts his eyes in my direction, then gives a smarmy smile. "I was just telling your nanny how wonderful it would be if she'd attend a party I'm throwing this weekend. Or next weekend." He tosses a wink at her that makes my stomach turn. "We're always partying down here in Malta. Aren't we, Keiran?"

"Some of us are working," I say, earning an eye roll from Louis and a gasp from Ella. Whatever. I'm not going to explain myself to this guy. I'm not going to spend another second talking to him if I don't have to. I take Ella's hand and offer Louis an insincere smile of my own. "If you'll excuse us? We were going to spend some time here on our private beach."

Yes, I emphasized the word *private*.

No, I don't care if that makes me a bad neighbor.

"Keir," Ella hisses as we walk away. "Why were you being so mean to that guy? He was nice."

"He's a creep," I mutter. "Probably just happy to have a pretty, young woman giving him the time of day."

"You think that guy was hitting on me?" She pulls her

114

hand away, giving me a funny look as she stops walking. "Are you crazy or just jealous?"

"I'm not jealous or crazy, thank you," I say, raising my voice and proving her right. "I was just trying to save you from getting dragged off to some swingers party where that old guy would try to do God-knows-what with you." I shrug as if it's no big deal, even though I'm practically shouting. "But by all means, go ahead and take him up on his offer if that's what you want to do."

"You really are acting crazy," she says, shaking her head. "What's gotten into you today? Why did you even come down here if you're just going to yell at me over something so stupid?"

I take a step back and shove a hand through my hair, trying to come up with an answer that doesn't make me sound like an asshole.

Yeah, I've got nothing.

"Where's Isla?" I ask instead. "I thought she'd be down here with you."

"She's taking a nap. Though she can probably hear you shouting from her bedroom."

I feel a stab of guilt at that thought. This is what Ella was talking about the other day, isn't it? This is why my daughter thinks we're mad at each other all the time.

Because I can't seem to keep my temper in check when I'm around Ella. Because I see her with another guy, even an old creep like Louis. I completely lose my shit.

That's a problem. I don't know how to solve it without completely cutting myself off from the situation.

From Ella.

"Ella?" Isla's little voice calls out from behind us, thankfully saving me from saying anything else that I might regret, even if she's sort of proving Ella's point at the same time.

"Dad? Why didn't you wake me up if you were coming to the beach?"

I don't know what to say, but Ella walks over to meet her with a smile and a hug. "We still have plenty of time to play on the beach, sweetie. Did you have a good nap?"

"I guess," Isla answers, tossing me a suspicious look over her shoulder as she walks by, hand-in-hand with Ella. "Can we build a sandcastle today?"

"Of course." Ella looks up at me as Isla squats down to gather up some sand. "Do you want to join us, Keir?"

I nod, feeling more like an asshole with each passing second. I love Ella, and she's fantastic with Isla, but this incident has been a sudden, painful reminder that all the reasons why we couldn't be together before are still present, bubbling just under the surface and waiting to sabotage any potential relationship.

She's too young. I'm too set in my ways. She wants a different life than the one I can provide. My family hates her.

Oh. Then there's the part where someone wants to kill her because of me.

A relationship is hard enough at the best of times. How is it supposed to survive all those challenges?

I don't think it can. I don't think any relationship could.

If this was a business decision, I would have already cut my losses and moved on to the next deal. Life isn't as black and white as business, though. And I'm not ready to cut my losses yet, even though I know it's the smartest thing I can do.

CHAPTER SEVENTEEN

ELLA

My mom sounds almost hysterical when I answer the phone. "Ella, dear? Is this a bad time?"

I'm alone in the living room, watching TV, but I look around just to make sure. "It's not a bad time for me. It has to be really early there, though. Is everything okay?"

"No, everything is," she sniffles, and it sounds like she's choking back a sob. "Everything is not okay. Not even close to being okay."

My heart is starting to beat faster as I stand up from the couch and start pacing. I'm already cursing myself for not being there to help with whatever new crisis has arisen at home while I've been away.

"Try to calm down," I say, even though I feel like I'm probably a few seconds away from a full-blown panic attack myself. "Just take a second and breathe." I try to follow my own advice, inhaling and slowly exhaling to calm my rattled nerves before I continue. "Now, tell me what's going on so I can try to help fix it."

"We're in trouble, Ella," she says, her voice trembling. "Financial trouble. The bank is threatening to take the house if we don't come up with a lot of money really soon."

I sit back down on the sofa, feeling the air rush from my lungs like I've just been punched in the gut. My family hasn't ever had much money. We don't have a lot of fancy things. That's fine. My parents taught me that my self-worth isn't tied to what I own or how much money I have in the bank. But they've always had that house. They've always been proud to be homeowners, to have that one tiny slice of the American dream.

"They can't just take the house," I say, even though I'm not entirely sure if that's true. "I think they have to give you a certain amount of notice. I'm sure they'd rather work with you to catch up on your payments than go through the hassle of foreclosing."

"They've given us notice," she says quietly. "It's gone past that point now, and we're almost out of time. I don't want to burden you with our troubles, but I don't know what else to do. Your father isn't sleeping. He's barely eating. He has too much stress right now as it is. I'm afraid this is going to push him over the edge. He's going to have a heart attack if something doesn't change."

"I know, Mom," I say, tears welling up in my eyes even as I'm trying to comfort her. "He's been so worried about Joy lately. I just don't know what to do. I want to help, but I don't even know where to start."

"Joy? Why has he been worried about Joy?"

"I—what?" I don't know what to say. Of course he's worried about Joy. Isn't she worried? Why does she sound so confused? Is she so upset that she can't think clearly? "Mom, maybe you should lie down or something. Have *you* seen a doctor lately? About your stress, I mean?"

She starts to answer, but the front door of the villa swings open, startling me and making me fumble with the phone as I crane my neck to see who it is.

"James?" I say it out loud, interrupting my mom and

probably confusing her even more than she already was. "Mom, I need to go. I promise I'll call you back and we'll get this figured out, okay? I love you."

I hang up the phone as Keir's brother strides into the living room. His eyes narrow as he looks at me. "Should have known I'd find you here. Where's Keir?"

I haven't seen James in a long time, but it hasn't been long enough to forget what a monster he is. The last time we were alone in a room together, he threatened me, then tried to get physical. I'm thankful there's some furniture standing between us this time, but I'm still ready to call out for help if he tries to pick up where we left off.

"He's in a meeting," I answer, keeping my eyes locked onto his as I fire off a question of my own. "What are you doing here? Is he expecting you?"

"I don't answer to the help," he snaps. "Anyway, I could ask you the same thing. I thought he left you at the airport."

God, I hate this man. Why is he always so nasty? What did I ever do to him?

"No, he didn't leave me there." I shift my weight away from him as he circles around to the side of the sofa. "We were almost killed that day. Someone came after us with a gun."

I'm sure he already knows the details, but I'm still a little unnerved by the way his expression hasn't changed. I might as well have been remarking on the weather.

"I heard," he says with a half-shrug. "Sounds like it was quite a spectacle. I'm sorry I missed it."

I can't stop myself from visibly recoiling as he takes a step closer. His eyes are dull and dead, like a shark. Like a predator. I wonder if he can sense the fear rolling off me in waves like a shark could.

"I know what you want from my brother," he continues, his lip curling up into a snarl. "You aren't going to get his money, though. Not while I'm still alive. So, why don't you do the smart, right thing? Why don't you go away? Hm? Go as far away as you can and stop scandalizing my family before something bad happens."

I can't breathe. I open my mouth to say something— anything—but no sound comes out. He's standing too close. I can see a flash of emotion in those dark eyes for the first time since he started talking.

Hatred.

He hates me. He also has the means and connections to do something about it. To make something bad happen, as he said.

And that scares me to death.

It's late in the evening when James leaves, and I have a chance to speak to Keir alone. I knock on his office door and ignore the annoyed look he shoots me when I step inside.

"It's been a long day, Ella," he says, sighing. "I hope you're not here to fight with me, too."

"Were you fighting with James?" I ask, already knowing his brother's visit is the reason for his foul mood. I'm just the lucky girl who gets to deal with the aftermath now that James is gone. "Did you know he was coming here today?"

"No. "I should have kicked him out, but," he pauses and wipes his brow with his hand. "But I didn't. I should have, but I didn't. Story of my life, right?"

He looks tired. Exhausted, really. I feel a moment of guilt for coming in here to question him when he's clearly had a rough day.

But I've had a rough day, too. Mostly thanks to his brother, though the phone call with my mom certainly didn't help matters.

"What did he want?" I press even though I know it isn't any of my business.

"He came here to ask me not to see you anymore. To beg me, actually."

The words hit me like a ton of bricks crashing down on top of me. "Are you serious? Why does he care so much about what we're doing? Why is he so hellbent on chasing me away?"

"He only cares about himself. His poll numbers are slipping. He thinks it's because you and I have been in the papers almost every day since we left Glasgow."

I'm still shocked James traveled all the way to Malta to beg Keir to break up with me, though I'm not entirely surprised. I should know by now that James is capable of anything that would serve his own self-interest.

"What did you say?" I'm almost scared to ask, but I have to know the answer.

"I told him not to blame his failing campaign on me. I asked him if he's ever considered the possibility that people just don't like him very much." Half a smile crosses Keir's lips. "That didn't go over very well."

I share his smile as I shake my head. "I can imagine. I should have guessed it had something to do with his campaign when he started in on me earlier."

Now it's Keir's turn to look concerned and ask questions. "What did he say? Do I even want to know?"

"It's nothing." I lie, making a dismissive gesture. "Nothing important, anyway."

I should probably tell him the truth, but what is he going to do about it? James is his brother. He'll probably be the next prime minister. Another confrontation between the two of them isn't the way to de-escalate this situation.

"He's going to stay in Malta for a few days," Keir says, making a face like he's just tasted something sour. "Since he decided to fly all the way down here. I guess he has to make it look like we're getting along, like we're one big, happy family."

"Great," I sigh, already steeling my nerves for the next time I'll have to see Keir's evil little brother. "Is it too late for me to catch a flight back to New York?"

I think he can tell that I'm only half-joking. His frown deepens as he shakes his head. "No way. I need you here. I need you even more now that my crazy family is around." He leans back in his chair and is quiet for a moment before he continues. "I won't stop you if you really want to go. But I hope you'll stay."

"I'll stay."

The words fall out of my mouth on their own, but what else was I going to say?

Of course I'm going to stay. We both know it. We both know why.

I love him.

CHAPTER EIGHTEEN

KEIR

It's nearly midnight when I softly knock on Ella's bedroom door. "Are you awake?" I whisper, opening it just enough to peer into the darkened room.

"I am now. What's going on?"

"Sorry, I thought you might still be up." Now I feel like an idiot and an asshole for waking her. "Never mind. I'll see you in the morning."

"Wait, Keir." She pushes her covers aside and walks over to the door to meet me. Wearing just an oversized t-shirt and no makeup, she's still the most beautiful woman I've ever seen. "What is it? I haven't been in bed for very long, and there's no way I'm getting back to sleep now unless you tell me what's wrong."

I hesitate a moment, my eyes traveling down to linger on her long, toned, dancer's legs. "I, uh…" Fuck. This seemed like a good idea when I was running it through my head. Now it seems stupid. "There's a movie playing at the cinema downtown that I thought you might want to see. There's a twelve-thirty showing tonight."

Her expression changes from concern to confusion in an

instant. "What? Tonight? "Twelve-thirty as in," she says, pausing to check the time. "Forty-five minutes from now?"

I nod. "Do you want to go?"

"Are you insane?" She laughs, then looks at the clock again. "And are you serious?"

"Yes and yes," I answer, trying not to join in with her laughter. "You don't need to put on any makeup because it's going to be dark in the theater anyway. We'll wear hats and glasses so nobody will recognize us."

'Are you serious?" she repeats. "You really want to take me to a movie now? In the middle of the night?"

I shrug. "I know it sounds crazy, but I figured we could both use a break. Isla is sleeping, and Mother is here if she needs anything. We'll only be gone a couple of hours, so we'll be back home before anyone wakes up and notices we're missing."

"This really is crazy," she says, moving away from the door and grabbing a pair of pants that are draped across the chair in the corner. "And I'm totally not dressing up, just for the record."

"That's fine. Perfectly fine. Like I said, we're going incognito."

We're sneaking out of the villa like two teenagers past curfew in fifteen minutes. "I haven't done something like this since boarding school," I confess. "I have to admit it feels a little silly."

"Probably because you're wearing sunglasses after midnight," she snorts. "So incognito."

Yeah, maybe I haven't thought this through very well.

Whatever.

I'm alone with Ella. That's the whole point of this dumb plan. So it's already a success in that regard. But I should probably still lose the sunglasses before I accidentally draw too much attention.

Malta isn't very big, thankfully, so it isn't a long walk from the villa to the center of the medieval town. Along the way, I point out a few of the more interesting sights, like the ancient church and one of the crusader castles.

"It's so beautiful," she's looking all around as we walk, taking in the sights and sounds of Malta at night. "So much history. It's weird to think that people have been walking along these same roads for hundreds of years. Thousands of years."

"That's right. It's a good reminder that we're only here for a short time. Makes me glad we're doing this together. I don't want to take a single second for granted while I'm with you."

"You say things like that, and it makes me wonder why we can't seem to overcome the things that are keeping us apart," she says, then huffs out a short breath. "I don't want to talk about that stuff right now, though. I didn't mean to bring it up."

I'm torn because I *do* want to talk about that stuff now that she's brought it up, but she's right. This isn't the right place or time. We're supposed to be having fun tonight, not putting our relationship through an existential crisis.

"We're almost there," I say, changing the subject and pointing down the winding, cobblestone road. "See the sign?"

She squints, then catches her breath when she sees the title of the movie we're going to see. "You're taking me to a ballet movie?" Her mouth drops open as she looks from the sign to me, then back again. "Really? Did Isla tell you I've been talking about seeing this movie?"

I laugh and shake my head. "I came up with this one on my own, believe it or not. I'm glad you're excited, though."

She's smiling from ear to ear. I'm relieved that our moment of tension seems to have completely passed. "I know it's going to be a super cheesy film. You're probably going to hate it. I really have been looking forward to seeing it ever since the trailer came out, though. There's this building in the trailer, I guess it's their dance studio. It's so beautiful. It's exactly the kind of place I could picture owning on the Upper West Side." She heaves a happy sigh, then continues. "It'll have ivy growing up the front of the building and little girls who look like me—girls of color, without any money—coming to learn ballet. That's my idea of heaven."

I'm not sure if she's still talking about the movie or her own dream studio, but I'm happy she's happy.

I also feel a twinge of sadness pulling at my heart as she paints a picture of that studio on the Upper West Side. This isn't the first time she's mentioned opening a place to teach young girls how to dance. She's obviously put a lot of thought into how she wants her future to look.

New York is a long way from Glasgow, though. it's hard not to notice that the future she's imagining doesn't seem to include me.

I won't ruin the night by pointing that out, but now the thought is stuck in my head. And even though I'm smiling and nodding as she rattles off the plot of the movie, I'm pretty sure I know exactly where my thoughts are going to be for the next couple of hours while we sit in the theater.

CHAPTER NINETEEN

ELLA

"I need you, Ella."

Those whispered words are all Keir has to say to bring me to my knees. I'm awake in my bed in the middle of the night when he says the magic words. I fling my covers back and beckon him to the bed. Scooting to the edge of the bed, I rise to meet him in the darkness.

The second he touches me, I'm lost.

Under Keir's hands, I shiver. I turn my face up to his, seeking his kiss. Keir's lips brush mine once, the most tentative of touches. I suck in a breath as I press up on my tiptoes, my hands gripping his shirt. I need him, need his lips to cover mine, to make me think of anything other than my leaving this bed.

And Keir obliges, god love him. He cradles my head and brings his head down again, meeting my mouth with hard, passionate kisses that leave me drugged and panting for more. He lies back on the bed and pulls me on top of his body in a single fluid movement. Keir's hand is on the small of my back, pushing my hips down as I straddle him.

The second the front of my panties makes contact with his lap, I moan. My whole body shudders because I have a glimpse into the future… a future that ends up with me coming like I've never come before. I nip at his full lower lip, begging him without words to get me to that peak.

Keir's fingers sink into my hair at the base of my neck, and he bucks up against me, a growl leaving his lips. "Fuck, Ella. I need you so badly. So fucking badly…"

The words skitter through my veins like an electric jolt. I can feel the distinct imprint of his cock through his slacks, pressing against me intimately. My mouth waters as I anticipate Keir filling me completely, taking my breath away, thrusting his cock so deep inside me that we both get lost. I feel a damp spot spreading across the front of my panties and I want more.

I need more of him, any way I can get him. The feeling is so strong that I'm almost dizzy with it.

Pushing myself upright, I rip at my dress, pulling it up over my head. My breasts bounce free for only a moment before Keir's hands come up to cover them, the roughness of his palms making me lose track of my thoughts. He shapes my breasts and tweaks my nipples at the same time. That small amount of stimulation makes the damp spot on the front of my panties widen considerably.

I open my mouth, a sound pouring out of my throat that is pure animalistic lust.

Keir slides his hands to my hips and pushes my body down and he thrusts up against me. He knows just how to get me horny beyond words, knows exactly what makes me moan.

My hands fall to his shirt and they rip at the buttons. I'm impatient, ready for him to slide inside me, to stretch me out.

"Keir!" I mutter, frustrated.

"What's the matter, darling?" he teases. "Whatever you want, I will do. Just name it, Ella."

I lick my lips, leaning down to press my lips against his,

snaking my tongue out to tease him. Keir's big hands press against my invasion, resisting my kiss.

"You know what I want. I want to hear you tell me just what you want me to do to you, sweetness."

Keir looks at me, his gaze falling to my breasts.

"I'm going to totally ruin you," he says quietly. "When I'm finished with you, darling, I'll leave nothing but burnt ruins."

I tremble because I know he's right. He removes his shirt, leaving me nearly stunned at his incredible state.

His stomach. Those are his biceps. His biceps are...

This guy is in amazing shape. It must take him hours and hours of practice every day to acquire such perfection. Muscle is ridged wherever I look.

"How do you keep your figure so trim?" As I enquire, my eyes widen.

As he unbuttons his black jeans, he glances at me. He kisses my neck while stroking my body with his lips.

"Wait till you see my cock," he quietly murmurs.

He kisses me while still wearing his pants. My heart is fluttering like a hummingbird in my chest. As he repositions me on the bed, a gasp leaves my lips, his hot kisses going down my neck and over my chest.

My breath comes to a halt in my chest as he licks his way down to my breast, yanking on one of my spaghetti straps and exposing my nipple. He smashes his venomous mouth into my breast, causing me to scream in agony as he sucks on it in long pulls.

The ache between my legs worsens and travels to my hips.

As he slides the second strap down, he releases go of my breast and wraps the slip around my waist. I'm nude under his hungry gaze, my hard nipples sticking openly between us.

His quick intake of breath is a siren's song to me. The sound of pure longing... I've never heard anything so enticing.

"You are so damn gorgeous," he cries, extending his fingers to shape the fullness of my breast. "Do you realize what you're doing to me, sweetheart?"

As I flush, my face and chest turn rosy. "I'm hoping you'll demonstrate..."

In response to my reaction, Keir quietly groans, stroking my lips. His lips brush against me, and his kiss is passionate, demanding, and desperate.

I move my fingers down his arm and touch his neck with my own hand. He moves his glance down my body as he draws back. I flush anew as a result of his frank scrutiny. It's tough to sit motionless when you're absorbed by his gaze like this.

He runs his hands down my sides, sensing the fullness of my hips, the beauty of his light skin against my dark figure. I gasp as he kisses me again, this time firmly and passionately. I feel nothing but pure, unrestrained passion.

It's amazing how much Keir makes me feel like I need him. Only him. He's the only one that can make me feel this beautiful and this desired.

I barely see him remove the silky slip until I'm down to my last garment, a little pair of sheer lace leggings. He nibbles his bottom lip, as if he's expecting something. I'm intrigued by his expression, expecting something unexpected to happen.

My excitement grows as a little, moist circle forms on the apex of my thighs on my panties.

Keir looks me in the eyes as he starts touching the wet triangle of fabric.

"Oh," I mumble, my voice choking. "Oh my goodness, that feels...

I let my eyes flutter shut as his skillful fingers began rubbing near my aching clit. Not touching it, but rubbing all around it. I force my eyes open to discover him looking at me, absorbing every feeling I express, and experimenting to find out what makes me the happiest.

His fingers continued to prod me through the damp fabric of my jeans. Even this much friction is incredible.

He kisses me, his tongue and lips as skilled as his fingers. I'm excited with excitement for him and what's to come. Everything else is secondary to how those fingers and tongue make me feel. I look up at him as he opens my thighs wide.

"Fuck!" he shouts, gliding his hands down my inner thighs. "You have the most gorgeous pussy I've ever seen, Ella."

He thumbs my slit oh so carefully, watching my expression. I close my eyes for a second and try to show him how incredibly turned on I am.

When I open my eyes again, Keir is looking at me with a smile on his face.

"Let's play some games." I need you to remain perfectly motionless. You are free to make as much noise as you like, but no hip-rocking or grabbing the sheets. "Do you believe you'll be able to handle it, sweetheart?"

I whine. "Keir... why don't you just fuck me already?"

"Maybe if you're good," he says.

I pull a face. He laughs, his fingers caressing my clit. I have to stop myself from bucking my hips up to meet his hand. A scorching moan of want and need escapes my lips.

"Good girl," he says softly as he moves down to kiss my throbbing, hungry clit. "Just like that. I love when you make noises, sweetheart."

Keir draws his fingertips down the seam of my pussy. When he pulls his fingers to his lips, glistening with the fluids of my desire, my mouth widens.

Is there anything sexier than Keir sucking my wetness off of his own fingers?

He stands up, his fingers going for his waist. With wide

eyes, I watch him unzip his trousers. He's bare underneath. His cock bursts free almost instantaneously, unimpeded by underwear.

My eyes is pulled to it like a bullseye. It's long, thick, and the perfect pink. My mouth waters and my pussy throbs.

He pulls his pants down and steps out of them completely. He's nude now, his thighs and hips as hard as the rest of him.

I flush and lay down on the bed. He leans in closer, allowing me to inspect him. So what's the harm? He doesn't have anything to hide.

When he finds my pussy with his fingers again, stroking up and down the slit in rhythmic caresses, his gaze latches onto mine.

In his brilliant blue eyes, I sense pure passion. I whisper small "mms" and "ohhhs" of delight as his hand travels rapidly.

As he bends forward, his cock rubs up against my.

When he gets closer, I open my mouth to kiss him, but he surprises me by murmuring in my ear.

He kisses an area on my neck, sucking hard enough to make me gasp. Keir then pulls away and falls on his knees, stunning me even more. Alarmed, I sit up partly, but he pulls me onto my back with firm hands against my stomach.

"I've been wanting to do this," he says softly, sliding his fingers up to part my pussy lips. "Putting my face in this creamy pussy. Hearing you moan. Eating you until you come on my tongue…"

He places a kiss against my clit between every sentence, a form of punctuation that I hadn't ever thought of but now don't know how I can live without.

"Keir," I whisper. A plea.

He presses the tip of his tongue against my exposed clit, which has been aching for a long time. It feels like a lightning bolt straight to my pleasure center, all my senses getting a fission of pure energy. For a minute, my breath is knocked out of my lungs as his tongue circles around my clit in steady circles.

I soon find myself burying my hands in his hair and bucking my hips against his tongue, in step with the rhythm he establishes. He comes to a complete halt for a split second, causing me to whimper.

"Be still," he orders. "Stay right there. Stay perfectly silent. As a reward, I'll continue to devour your pussy."

I stifle a moan and nod, bracing myself. I manage to stay motionless as my pussy throbs, needy. My face is hot, my entire body a ball of desire.

I need Keir's magical tongue on my fucking clit right the fuck now.

Without a word, Keir starts over, rekindling the fire and letting me feel sensations I've never felt before.

I can feel my body begin tightening, feel the beginning of the upward climb to my peak. I never imagined that somebody could instill such a desire in me. But I'm willing to beg him to continue.

I plow my hands into his hair, his name on my lips, my back bowing against the bed.

It's so wonderful when Keir sucks and licks at my clit that my entire body is on fire. He closes his lips around my clit and sucks. I'm at the very edge of sanity, clinging to it by a thread.

He moans into my body, a tidal wave crashing into me, filling my entire body up with sensation. An inarticulate sounds leaves my lips and my body spasms, bucking. I come apart, grasping his hair with a shudder and a deep groan. He slowly licks and kisses my clit until I stop him, putting my hands between my body and that invasive, magical tongue.

I bring him up to my chin and kiss him hard. He tastes

like ozone with a hint of sweetness. With a surprise, I realize I'm tasting myself on his lips and tongue.

"What do you want me to do now, sweetheart?"

I reach for his cock, gently pulling Keir against my body. I bite my lower lip and rub my soft, wet pussy against his firm, hot cock. "Fuck me, please."

The wicked grin he gives me is almost enough to undo me. Keir grabs my hips and positions himself, standing between my legs

I'm still moist from what he just did with his mouth, but even the slightest bit of pushing his cock inside stretches me out. Even though I desire him, my body is resisting.

I gasp. "Oh my god. Your cock is so big, Keir. I love the way you stretch me out."

Our bodies connect as he works his hips in and out of me. I close my eyes and relax into his massive cock's thrusts. It's raw and hot, passionate and sexy. I clench my innermost muscles around his cock, enjoying the way he hisses.

"Fuck, sweetheart. Your pussy feels so goddamn good," he says through clenched teeth.

I draw Keir in, circling my arms around his shoulders and rubbing my heels over his ass and back. I try to meet his thrusts with my own, watching his face as his thrusts grow quicker and more heated.

"Look at me, Ella," he says firmly. "I want you to watch me while I come. I want you to see how you make me fucking feel."

So I do. I look up into his eyes, the coil of my yearning tightening inch by inch. Raking my nails down his back and following his thrusts with my own, I believe I have never been closer to another person than I am to Keir right now. I kiss him, kiss his neck, kiss his shoulders.

"Fuck," he mumbles. "I'm obsessed with you, Ella. I want to watch you come when I do. We'll burn together."

His words ignite my very soul. "Oh, Keir..."

As I watch, his expression turns to one of the most exquisite torture. "Come for me, sweetheart. Show me what a good fucking girl you are."

I begin to fracture, spasming as I come. He's right behind me, meeting my every thrust, kissing me feverishly, finding my hand and clutching it so tightly that I'm scared it'll break.

He comes with a shiver, hammering me mercilessly. I can feel him pulsating within me.

Keir kisses me with a breathless wonder. I return his kiss, wrapping my arms around his neck. We lie like that for a long time. My breathing slows. His does too.

Before I know it, I am pulled down into a deep sleep, still laying in his arms.

CHAPTER TWENTY

KEIR

I've had a restless, mostly sleepless two nights. Ever since my midnight date with Ella, she's all I've been thinking about.

Except not in the horny, greedy, needy way I normally think about her. I've been anxious, annoyed, and grouchy.

Grumpier than normal, as Isla informed me at dinner last night.

So the last person I want to see waiting for me in the kitchen when I come downstairs for coffee this morning is my brother.

"Who let you in?" I grumble in place of a greeting as I reach for the coffee pot.

"Security."

"Figures. It's time to fire the security team. Again."

I swear to God, it's a miracle any of us are still alive after dealing with these so-called bodyguards. I'm half-joking with James, but I'm seriously going to have a word with those guys when he leaves.

"Anyway," his gaze follows me around the kitchen as I go about my morning routine of adding sugar to my coffee, toasting the bread, and buttering the toast. Catching up on the emails I received while I was asleep. "Do you have any urgent meetings this morning?"

"Three," I answer, still reading. "Maybe four."

"Can you reschedule one or two of them?"

I look up from my phone and frown. "Why? Can't you tell me whatever it is now. save us both some hassle? Since I know you didn't just stop by to say hi and see my smiling face this morning."

"I'd be disappointed on both counts," he smirks, looking around. "And I'd rather wait until we're behind closed doors to talk, if that's okay with you."

I thought I just made it clear that it isn't okay with me, but it's too early to argue. Besides, I know he'll keep arguing until he gets his way, since that's what he always does.

Pointing toward my office with my phone in one hand while I grab my coffee with the other, I mentally try to prepare myself for whatever fresh hell my brother is about to put me through. "Let's make this quick, at least. I really do have to sit in on a couple of those meetings this morning."

Once we're in my office and I've had a chance to sit down at my desk and take a sip of coffee, I notice he's acting strange. Stranger than usual. Fidgety and nervous, which I'm pretty sure are the first traits they beat out of you in prime minister prep class or whatever it is he took at Eton.

"What's the matter with you?" I ask, studying him as he paces around my office. "And sit down, will you? You're freaking me out."

"I'm sorry," he says as he slumps into an armchair across from my desk. "I've hardly slept since I've been here."

"That makes two of us. What's your excuse? Partying? Scheming to take over the world? Planning your redecoration of Number Ten Downing Street?"

"Funny. I won't ever be moving into Number Ten at this

rate. My campaign is losing steam. We have been for some time now."

That isn't exactly news to me. I've seen the polling and read the headlines about my brother's bid to become the next leader of the U.K., and while he'll likely have an easy time winning his seat in parliament, his status as the future leader of the party and country is very much still up in the air.

"All campaigns have ebbs and flows," I say, shrugging. "Maybe you've had a couple of unfavorable news cycles, but that'll turn around."

"I don't think it will. First of all, it's been more than a couple of unfavorable cycles. My name is constantly in the papers. not for the reasons my campaign would prefer."

Should I feel guilty? My situation with Ella is almost certainly contributing to those shitty headlines, but I'm finding it hard to muster an apology for something that shouldn't be anyone's business in the first place.

"I'll try to cut back on how often I'm photographed with Ella," I say, giving him that small concession even though I'm already chafing at the prospect of going back into hiding. "That should bump your poll numbers up a percentage or two."

He snorts and almost smiles. "I appreciate the thought, but you and Ella are the least of my problems right now. Within the party, leak after leak has occurred. All the scandals are adding up. The voters can see there's a lack of leadership. it doesn't help that all they're hearing is this steady trickle of bad news out of Westminster." He shakes his head and looks up at the ceiling for a moment before meeting my gaze again. "You know I don't like to ask for help, but I'm at my wits' end, Keir. I don't know what to do. My advisers aren't help-ing. They think the solution to every problem is to throw more money at it."

"Will that help?" I offer. "Throwing money at the problems? Because I can write a check if that's what you need."

No, I shouldn't be helping him at all.

Yes, I'm angry with myself for even offering.

But he's my only brother. I don't know if I can forgive him for some of the crazy shit he's pulled recently, but I'm too old and too tired to spend the rest of my life hating him.

"I'm not sure," he says with a frown. "Maybe? More money is almost always a good thing. I'm just not sure if it's worth it. You get zero return on investment if I lose. it's looking like that's the direction we're heading."

I don't think I've ever seen James go through a crisis of confidence. Even when he's unsure about something, he almost always bluffs his way through. And it almost always works.

But this sad, anxious, dejected look is a new one for him. It's honestly starting to worry me a little.

"Come outside with me," I say, standing up so abruptly that it takes a few seconds for him to follow. "The fresh air might do some good."

"Certainly can't hurt," he agrees, following me out onto the patio and then down the steps to the beach. "So what do you think I should do? Aren't big brothers supposed to have all the answers?"

"I do have all the answers." I shoot him a half-grin as he catches up to me. "You're just asking all the wrong questions. Let's start by establishing what you want to do. That's the important part in all this. Do you even want to be prime minister?"

The furrow in his brow and the hesitation before he answers tell me everything I need to know. "I thought I wanted it. I used to want it. Now, I'm not so sure."

"The leadership your party is looking for has to come from you," I continue. "You understand that, right? If you don't feel like you can be the leader of the party, not to mention the entire country, then you need to suspend your campaign. Put those poor bastards who are volunteering for you out of their misery."

"I sort of brought that idea up with our parents last week," he confesses. "I'm sure you can imagine how that dinner went."

I wince. "Yeah, I can imagine. That explains Mother's shitty mood lately."

He snorts. "Hey, I can't take all the credit for that. She's been pulling her hair out because of you."

Is it wrong that I'm smiling? Is it more wrong that I'm happy James is taking some of the heat off me for once? I'm sure the pendulum will swing back in my direction eventually, but for now, it's kind of nice knowing that I'm not the only one on our parents' shit list.

"You know I can always make a spot for you at News-Corp, right?" I swore I'd never let my brother step foot back in our corporate offices, but that feels like so long ago. I'm not sure how much has actually changed since then, but I want to believe James can be a good, decent human at least some of the time. "There would be a few provisions in your contract, of course."

"Such as?"

He's interested. That's a good sign.

"A morality clause, for starters. If you even so much as glance sideways at a female employee, I'll fire your ass and expose you in the media so fast your head will spin."

"Let me speak with my campaign manager, but," he swallows hard and stares me down. "I want to take you up on that offer. And I appreciate it, Keir. I really do."

"It's no problem." I clap him on the back and pull him in for a half-hug. "That's what big brothers are for, right? We should probably keep this plan to ourselves for a while, though. At least until we're ready to go ahead with it. No sense in giving Mother a coronary."

"She'll probably know before I even leave the property."

He says it in such a nonchalant way that his words take a second to sink in. "What do you mean? You're not going to tell her, are you?"

"No, but," he says, cocking his head to one side. "You really don't know?"

I don't like where this conversation is going. I'm quickly losing my patience. "No," I say slowly, trying to tamp down the irritation that's rising up inside me. "But you can go ahead and fill me in on what the fuck you're talking about anytime."

Now he looks worried. "I just assumed you knew," he says, glancing back over his shoulder. "The villa is probably bugged, for starters."

"No." I shake my head. "I... no. I don't believe that."

"Why do you think Mother keeps it in her name? Why do you think she lets you stay here?" He sighs as my mouth falls open. "Even if it isn't—and I'm telling you, it is—there's also the deal with your security team."

My throat is starting to close up, and my irritation instantly turns to pure anger at the mention of my security people. "What about them?"

"I swear, I thought you knew." He looks like it's actually hurting him to say the words as he continues. "They report to Mother and Father. Everywhere you go. Every move you make. They used to report to me, too, but only because some of them were on my campaign's payroll, if you'll recall."

Jesus.

"What the fuck?" is all I can say. "You've been spying on me all this time? You've been in on it with them?"

"You can't be this shocked, Keir," he says, giving me a skeptical look. "Or this stupid. Of course they've been keeping tabs on you. They spy on me, too. That just goes with the territory." He shakes his head. "Did you forget who your family is?"

My head is spinning. I need to sit down, but there's nothing to hold onto out here on the beach. "I can't believe this. I seriously had no idea."

"You didn't question why your security guy took care of Max? You didn't wonder who gave that order, did you?"

When I don't answer, he mouths a single word that sends a chill up my spine. "*Mother.*"

Holy shit.

James just accused my mother of conspiracy to commit murder and implicated himself at the same time.

She had Max killed. James knew about it.

"What about Ella?" I clench my fists, ready to swing at him if he gives me the wrong answer. "Did she give that order, too?"

He holds his hands up in surrender and takes a step back. "I don't know anything about that, Keir. I only heard about it after the fact. I swear to God I didn't have anything to do with it."

His answer is convincing enough to save his ass for now. Barely. But it still isn't the answer I'm looking for.

"What. About. Mom?" I ask, emphasizing each word.

"I don't know," he says again. "You'll have to ask her yourself. I wouldn't, though."

"Oh, I'm going to ask her. I'm going to get the truth one way or another."

"You know she won't admit to it. She'll lie and try to turn it around on you." He pinches the bridge of his nose and squeezes his eyes shut for a moment. "Or she'll just blame it all on me. She'll never take responsibility for the things she's done to either of us over the years. You might as well save your breath. Just make sure that you're really, truly alone if you're going to say something you don't want people to hear."

I don't usually find myself at a loss for words, but James has accomplished that feat. "Thanks for the heads-up, I guess," I manage, feeling like the wind has been knocked out of me. "I'll hold onto that information for now."

Only for now, though.

When the time is right, I'm going to confront our mother about what she knows and what she's done.

And God help her if she's the one who has been trying to hurt Ella.

CHAPTER TWENTY-ONE

ELLA

The Maltese sun is beating down on us as we sit down outside at a cafe for lunch. "I thought we weren't allowed to be seen out in public," I say, shielding my eyes from the sunlight as I look over at Keir. "Your family won't be pleased if anyone sees us."

"They can go to hell," he says with a shrug. "I don't care what my family thinks right now."

I don't try to hide my surprise. "Since when? What about upholding the family name and all that stuff?"

I'm not sure what's caused his sudden change of heart, but I like it so far. The less pressure Keir is under, the better our chances are of having a somewhat normal relationship.

As normal as a world-famous billionaire can get, I guess.

"Since my brother came over this morning, and--" he pauses and casts a scowl over my shoulder. "Damned paparazzi. They really are everywhere. Like fucking roaches."

I lean in closer, doing my best to ignore whatever sideshow the paparazzi are setting up behind me. "Since your brother came over, and what?" I prompt, hoping he'll get back to whatever he was about to say. "What did he do?"

"Hm?" Keir slowly turns his attention back to me, but is still keeping one eye on the photographer behind me. "He stated that my mother and father employ the entire security detail. Including, I'm guessing, the guy who chased and terrified you at the airport."

I gape at him. "What?"

Keir swats at a paparazzo, even though I can't see the one he's concerned with. I'm guessing the guy must be across the small cobblestone street, but I know he'll have an easier time taking our picture if I turn to look. Still, it's more than a little unnerving to know that every move we make is being followed so closely.

We've only just arrived at the cafe. There are already people starting to notice us. Granted, word gets around fast on a small island, but this is different. This feels more intrusive.

And maybe it's just my imagination, but there's also a tension in the air that I don't normally notice. Or maybe it has to do with the fact that Keir is growing more and more agitated and angry every time his gaze flicks over in that direction.

"Try to ignore them," I murmur. I start to reach over for his hand before I catch myself and grab my water glass instead. "What do you know about the security detail?"

"Nothing definitive. But James was quite willing to give up details about my mother's involvement in Max's murder."

"What!?" I gasp. "You can't be serious!"

"I'm serious as the death sentence. By my brother's accounting, my mother has a lot of blood on her hands. Of course, I haven't verified this with anyone else. So he could be full of it. But it may very well be true."

I shake my head, pushing back my hair. "I know your mother is rude and doesn't follow the rules... but to think she's a murderer? I can't believe you let James keep talking."

Keir shrugs, distracted by something out of my field of vision. He pushes to his feet just as I turn to see three reporters snapping photos.

"Keir," I begin, but he shakes his head.

"Just a second, Ella. I'm sorry." He scoots closer to me and places a protective hand on the back of my chair as he looks up over the top of my head. "Don't come any closer. You've taken your photos; now get the hell out of here and leave us alone."

It's impossible to resist looking now. I can sense the other man nearby even if I can't see him right away, but I'm not prepared for just how close he is when I finally glance back over my shoulder and hear the unmistakable click and whir of his camera.

"Lord," I turn away from him as quickly as I can, but I know it's too late. "These guys really have no shame at all, do they?"

"They're the worst," Keir agrees before raising his voice again. "Go. Away. I'm not going to warn you again." He adds a small gesture this time, as if swatting a fly.

I hear the guy say something that sounds a lot like Keir's favorite curse word, just in Italian. There's a venom in the stranger's voice that surprises me all over again, but I'm trying my best to take my own advice and ignore him.

Don't let them ruin our lunch.

Don't let them ruin our lunch.

"You want to say that a little louder, asshole?" Keir calls out. "Wanna tell me to fuck off without that camera protecting your face?"

Too late. Lunch has officially been ruined.

The guy says something else I can't understand, and Keir rises up from his seat. "Keir, please," I whisper, reaching for his arm and hoping to calm him down. "Maybe we should

146

just leave. He's just trying to taunt you. Let's not give him the satisfaction of knowing it's working."

Again, it's too late. I might as well be talking to the medieval brick wall behind him.

"Fuck this guy," Keir growls, lunging past me and startling a scream from the woman at the table next to us.

The photographer is yelling in Italian now, stumbling backwards but still documenting every move Keir makes. I can't even imagine how damaging these photos are going to be or the fallout Keir will have to endure with his family, his business, and the general public, who already don't have a super high opinion of him.

I have to stop this madness. It's already gotten way out of hand, but maybe we can still salvage our day and what's left of Keir's reputation if we leave now.

"Let's go," I say, coming up behind Keir and taking his arm. "Please, let's just get out of here."

I might actually be breaking through his anger this time. He nods slightly and takes a step back with me, but stops again, and his eyes go wide as he shifts his weight and tries to tuck me behind him. "Get down, Ella. Now!"

But I'm too slow to react. I look up just in time to see the guy charging at us with his fists raised. I duck, and Keir blocks him from colliding with me, but I can still feel a sharp pain explode in my cheek as the stranger's fist makes contact.

I scream and fall, scrambling to get away while Keir grapples with the photographer. Keir throws a punch, then another, and another, until he's on top of the man. "Is this what you want?" Keir roars, hitting the guy again. "Was the picture worth getting beat up for? Worth hitting a woman?"

Blood is spraying from the guy's nose, and I'm afraid Keir will kill him if he doesn't stop. I pick myself up and hurry over, tugging at Keir's shoulder just before he slugs the guy again.

"Let's go," I say, my cheek throbbing with every move I make. I can already feel my eye swelling up. I don't even want to think about how bad this is going to look when it's all over. I just want to get the hell out of here. "Now, Keir. We have to leave."

He looks up at me, and his whole demeanor changes. "Shit," he says, leaving the guy in the street and taking me into his arms instead. "I'm so sorry, Ella. I tried to protect you. I swear I tried."

There's no time for any of this right now. "We have to go," I repeat, still tugging at him even though his strong arms are finally wrapped around me completely. "Keir, come *on*."

"Right," he nods, finally coming to his senses and ushering me back to the table so we can collect our things. "We need to leave before the police get here. I'll call a doctor for you on the way back to the villa."

I don't think I need a doctor, but I'm not going to bother trying to talk him out of it. We have more important things to worry about right now, like trying to get home without being arrested for assault and battery.

CHAPTER TWENTY-TWO

KEIR

It's been almost twenty-four hours, but I still feel horrible for what happened. I can't look at Ella without regretting every single one of my actions yesterday, but she hasn't complained at all.

Even when we were kicked out of Malta, she found the silver lining in the situation by saying how much she missed Drummond Castle and how happy she would be to see it again.

She's a fighter. She's an angel. She's my saving grace. I love her, even if I'm still scared to admit it out loud.

"I wish you'd stop looking at me like that," she says, taking the cup of tea that I've prepared for her and wincing as she lifts the cup to her lips. "I know I look like a monster. I'm reminded every time I try to move. Or speak. Or breathe."

"You don't look like a monster," I say, sitting down on the sofa next to her. "Do you want me to get you something for the pain? I can have the doctor come back and prescribe some pills."

"No," she says, giving me a half-smile from the side of her face that isn't swollen. "I don't need any pills. It was just one punch. I'm pretty sure you blocked most of it. I'd hate to think what I might look like if he'd hit me square in the face."

I can feel myself getting angry all over again as I replay the scene in my mind. How the guy was taunting us. How the feeling of rage clouded my judgment. How something ugly inside me took over when I realized he'd hurt Ella.

I don't recognize the person I turned into yesterday, but I don't regret hitting the guy. I don't regret sending him to the hospital after what he did to Ella.

To *my* Ella.

"He looks ten times worse," I say, trying to push those thoughts aside and focus on what really matters right now. Her. "I'm so sorry this happened. It's one hundred percent my fault. I should have listened when you tried to get me to leave. We could still be in Malta right now if I'd ignored that son of a bitch."

"You can't beat yourself up over that," she says, then flashes me another lopsided grin. "No pun intended. Seriously, though, you don't have to keep apologizing. You're not the one who hit me. You were trying to protect me from getting hurt."

"I'm still the reason you got hurt in the first place." I put an arm around her shoulders and pull her in closer. "So yes, I do need to keep apologizing. I *will* keep apologizing until you get back to normal. then I'll apologize a few more times for good measure."

"I appreciate the gesture, even if it isn't necessary." She leans against my shoulder, her body melting against mine. "This is why I love—"

She stops herself mid-sentence, her whole body tensing up. Neither of us seems ready to fully say those words out loud, but it makes my heart do a slow roll in my chest to know that we both feel the same way about each other.

"You don't have to finish that sentence," I whisper,

planting a kiss on the top of her head as the tension leaves her body. "I think you know I have feelings for you, too."

She is stiff in my arms, but she slowly nods her head. That's all the confirmation I need. She loves me. She loves me, even though I've acted like a jerk, like a caveman attempting and failing to protect her. That thought warms me inside, filling a space in my chest I thought had long since gone dead.

It's an odd feeling. I force my mind to think of something else, anything else, lest I obsess about the fact that she loves me. My head swivels around, and I focus on my surroundings.

It's strange to be back at the castle after spending so much time away. I never thought I'd miss the gray skies or the quiet solitude, but there's a comfort in being able to look out the window and not see another human for miles in any direction.

After having to deal with the paparazzi for weeks on end, I find it especially comforting to look out my window and see the Highlands.

Fuck, I still can't believe I let them get to me like that. I let my guard down, and now Ella has paid the price. It's unbelievable and inexcusable. I'll never, ever let it happen again.

I walk over to check that she's still resting comfortably in the sitting room, then walk down the corridor to the office I've set up here in the castle. It's the one high-tech area of the centuries-old estate, but today I'm seriously regretting the wall of television screens plastered with my angry face and the multiple phone lines all lighting up with reporters' questions.

How long until this shit show dies down? Yes, I probably deserve some public backlash after the way I acted in Malta, but they've conveniently left out the part where Ella and I had been hounded by those jackasses for weeks and weeks until we'd finally been pushed past the breaking point. They've also left out the way the guy was taunting me and the way he caught Ella with a left hook.

Putting it all in context, most people might not be surprised that I lost my temper. Most reasonable people probably would have done the same thing.

Context doesn't matter, though. All that matters are clicks, views, and sensational headlines. Ironically, it's my own media empire that's leading the charge against me. The worst, most salacious headlines are coming from news outlets that I own.

I walk over to my desk and pick up the phone, dialing the familiar number of the NewsCorp headquarters in Glasgow without thinking.

"Benny," I say when the UK News Director's voice greets me. "Put me in contact with a reporter. A friendly reporter."

I hang up and wait, but not for long. My phone rings again almost immediately. Does it blur a few ethical lines for the person in charge of news programming to help me leak a few favorable stories?

Probably.

Do I care?

Not even a little.

Why else would I keep paying his extortionate salary?

When I answer the phone, I'm relieved to hear a genuinely friendly voice on the other end of the line.

"Good to speak to you again, Lord Greyrose. I don't know if you remember me, but I'm Evan O'Connell with the Times."

"Of course," I sigh relievedly as I settle into my chair at my desk. "How have you been, Evan?"

"Well enough, thank you. I would ask the same, but I've seen the unfortunate news coming out of Malta."

"Indeed," I sigh. "That's why I wanted to speak to

someone here, someone from Scotland who knows me a little better than the foreign press."

"I appreciate that you thought of me, sir," he continues. "And I'll be happy to help you get your side of the story out there for the public to hear."

I spend the next thirty minutes telling Evan more information about my personal life than anyone has a right to know, but it's a necessary trade-off if I'm going to have any chance of recovering from this self-induced crisis.

"And you are officially divorced now?" he asks. "That's on the record?"

"Correct. It was amicable, and we've agreed that our daughter should stay with me for the majority of the time."

Most of this is true. A divorce is less than amicable, of course, but nobody actually admits how brutal those hearings really are.

"Can you tell me if there's any truth to the rumors that you've been having an affair with your daughter's nanny for the past several months?"

Ouch.

That's a less-than-friendly question, isn't it? At least he's giving me the opportunity to answer directly, though.

I take a deep breath, buying myself a few more seconds to collect my thoughts. "First, I want to be completely clear that even though my divorce has just recently been finalized, my ex-wife and I have been legally separated for over a year. Almost a year and a half. I stayed faithful to my wedding vows until we both decided that the marriage was irretrievably broken. Even then, I didn't start dating when I could have because I didn't want to risk upsetting or confusing my daughter."

"Yes, sir," he answers. "I'll make sure that's clearly stated in the article I write. But I'd be remiss in my journalistic duties if I didn't point out that you haven't actually answered my question."

Shit.

I know better than to think I can dazzle an experienced, veteran reporter with my title and wealth, but I'm still secretly hoping he'll cut me a little slack on the relationship issue.

Apparently, there's only so much slack he's willing to give.

"I am seeing someone," I answer through clenched teeth. "That's all I'll say."

"Your daughter's nanny?"

"That's all I'll say," I repeat. "Thank you for your time, Evan. I hope I haven't kept you too long."

"Not at all, sir," he says, mercifully dropping the uncomfortable question about Ella. "Thank you for reaching out. I'm only a phone call away if you ever want to talk again."

He says it in such a relaxed way that it's almost easy to forget he's being paid to print all this information about me.

I hang up the phone and ease back into my chair, closing my eyes and hoping I've made the right decision. Going to the press and giving an interview about my personal life is a dangerous gamble at the best of times.

Evan O'Connell has the power to help turn the tide of public opinion back in my favor. But he could just as easily use my words against me if that's what he decides to do.

God knows I've given him plenty of ammunition.

CHAPTER TWENTY-THREE

ELLA

There's a lot of activity at the castle today. I'm trying not to be too nosy.

Okay, I'm actually not trying that hard. I'm being nosy.

But Keir has hired a new personal assistant. That means I'll be working with someone new on a regular basis. I think I'm entitled to do a little snooping, just to find out what kind of person he's hired to fill such an important role.

It seems reasonable to me, at least.

I get my first look at the assistant just before Keir whisks her—*her*—away into his office.

I'm not impressed.

Or maybe I am impressed. That's the problem. God, am I the one getting jealous now?

Granted, I haven't officially met the woman yet, but I can tell from looking at her that she's professional, classy, and pretty.

Really pretty.

Fine.

I'm jealous.

That's valid. I'm allowed to have these feelings as long as I don't let them cloud my judgment. She's probably perfectly nice, in addition to all her other good qualities, so I'm not going to be rude or petty when I finally get a chance to meet her.

But I will keep an eye on her until I know for sure what her intentions are. Lord. Now I sound like Keir's brother. Or his mother.

I shudder at the realization that I'm uncomfortably close to passing judgment on this new hire, just like Keir's relatives passed judgment on me.

I'll just have to trust him. Which… I *do*. For all his flaws, he's never once given me a reason to think he's interested in anyone else. Not ever.

Still, I can't help but wonder if there's a reason he hired this particular woman. I don't doubt that she was probably the most qualified candidate. Keir sometimes thinks with his dick, but that isn't how he runs his business. That's James's specialty, from what I understand.

But this woman is objectively pretty. Objectively beautiful, really. There's no way that didn't factor into his decision. He's human, after all.

I huff out a short breath and sit down on the couch while I give Keir's office door the evil eye.

Okay, I need to stop.

Seriously.

I'm not going to let myself turn into this jealous, insecure monster. I'm going to keep my insecurities locked up tight, like a normal person. And that means I'm going to give this woman a fair shake. I'll wait to pass judgment until after I've met her. then I'll keep my feelings to myself.

Unless Keir asks what I think, of course.

The sound of the butler clearing his throat pulls me from my thoughts. "There's someone here to see you," he says, gesturing toward the great hall.

"Me?" I look around the empty sitting room as if he could be talking to someone else.

"I asked if you were expecting him, but he wouldn't answer. He's, ah," he says, pausing and raising a brow. "Quite insistent."

I don't like the sound of this. "No, I'm not expecting anyone," I say as I stand up and start following him through the house. "Do you know who it is?"

He turns and gives me a curious look right before we make it to the hall. "I believe it's your father."

That's the only warning I get before I find myself face-to-face with my dad. "What? Dad?" I seriously can't believe my eyes right now. It feels like someone is playing a prank on me. "What are you doing here? How did you even get here?"

"Don't look so surprised," he snaps, craning his neck to look past me. "I warned you. I told you to stop stalling. Now I'll have to take matters into my own hands. Where is he? Where's Keiran?"

"I don't know," I lie, starting to panic. "What are you talking about? Tell me why you're here."

This is bad. Very bad. Catastrophic.

I've done my best to ensure this day would never come, but here it is. Here we are, all under the same roof. How am I going to explain this to Keir? He's going to see my dad here and think I invited him. He's going to think I wanted this to happen.

I have to get to him first. I turn to look for the butler, but he's already gone. When I turn back to face my dad, he's stepping around me, apparently determined to go looking for Keir on his own.

"Dad, stop," I say, hurrying to block his way. "Please, just talk to me for a second, okay? Tell me what's going on. Or better yet, let's go somewhere else and talk. Somewhere private."

"You'd like to hide me away again, wouldn't you?" he sneers. "Not gonna happen. Not this time. Not until after I've had a conversation with your boyfriend."

Oh, God.

I feel like I'm going to throw up or pass out. Or maybe both. I'm starting to sweat, and my stomach feels like it's in my throat.

Keir's voice behind me makes it ten times worse. "What's going on here? Ella? Why is your dad here?"

My father answers before I have a chance to say anything. "You don't need to ask her. You can talk to me, man to man. Unless you're afraid?"

"Stop," I whisper, but it's too late. This is really happening. I look into my dad's glassy, crazed eyes, but he's not paying any attention to me. "Please don't do this."

"Who do you think you are?" Keir demands. "Barging into my home and insulting me? My respect for Ella is the only thing keeping me from throwing you out of here right now, sir, but don't test my patience."

Dad barks out a harsh laugh. "Your respect for her? That's a joke, right? The whole world knows you've been fucking the nanny, and she's been using you for your money." He sneers as he looks from Keir to me. "Or did you finally get him to believe that you were in love? I thought there was no way he could be that stupid." His gaze flicks back to Keir. "Now I think maybe I was wrong."

I wish the floor would open up and swallow me. I wish I could rewind time and stop this whole messy scene from ever happening. Most of all, I wish I could take back every angry word I've said about Keir to my family. I wish I could take back all the times I indulged my dad's crazy rants and all the promises I've made to help him out of his financial mess.

If I'd ever dreamed this would happen—that my worst

nightmare would come true—I never would have made those promises. I never would have spoken to him at all.

"What's he talking about, Ella?" I turn to see Keir looking at me, his face a mask of anger and confusion. "Why did he say you were trying to convince me you were in love?"

"It's not like that," I start to say, but my dad cuts me off again.

"It's exactly like that," he shouts. "Just like that. Go ahead and ask her. See if she'll lie to your face. Ask her if she planned on using you for your money."

Please no.

Please don't ask.

"Did you?" The inevitable question hits me like a punch to the stomach. "Was that what you were planning?"

I don't try to stop the tears from rolling down my cheeks as I plead with him. "It was never my idea, Keir. You have to believe me. I only ever agreed to his plan because my sister needs expensive treatments for her cancer. I swear that's the only reason, but I couldn't do it. I couldn't take your money. I didn't want to do it."

I'm babbling and sobbing as my whole world crashes down around me. Keir and my dad are both yelling, and I'm caught in the middle.

"See?" Dad points at me, a deranged smile spreading across his face. "I told you. She was ready to take your money and run." He laughs again and shakes his head. "Ella, you've really messed up now. And for what?"

"To help Joy," I swipe at the tears, but they keep falling. "That was all I ever wanted to do."

"You really are an idiot, aren't you? Joy doesn't have cancer. That was just part of the plan, not that it matters anymore. But I'm sure she'll appreciate your loyalty when she finds out how hard you worked on her behalf."

I can't breathe. I need to sit down. I stagger toward the

wall, barely able to keep my legs from giving out. This is, by far, the worst day of my life. And the hits just keep coming.

Everything has been a lie. I've agonized over what to do and how to help my sister for weeks. Months.

All for nothing.

I'll never forgive my dad for doing this to me. For putting me in this position. Never.

"Get him out of here," Keir says. I can hear several sets of boots on the stone floor as my dad shouts incoherently.

I'm not watching any of it, though. My field of vision has narrowed, and I seriously think I might be on the verge of passing out. I'm just leaning against the wall, waiting for this torture to end.

When it's finally quiet again, I turn to look at Keir. All the color has drained from his face. there's nothing but pain in his eyes as he meets my gaze.

"Keir, I'm sorry. I—"

"No," he interrupts, his deep voice barely above a whisper. "Don't speak to me."

I close my mouth and watch as he walks out of the room.

It's over.

I've lost him.

And it's my own fault.

CHAPTER TWENTY-FOUR

KEIR

It's been too long since I've made an appearance at the NewsCorp headquarters. There's a mountain of paperwork on my desk and a stack of messages that will take me weeks to get through, but that's fine.

I have all the time in the world. I sure as hell don't want to go back home.

"How could she have done that?" I inquire aloud to my empty office. "How could she betray my trust like that?"

I've asked myself those same questions a million times while I drove from the castle to my office in Glasgow, but I still haven't come up with any good answers.

Maybe there isn't a logical, reasonable answer at all. Maybe I don't know anything about the woman who has been living under my roof and taking care of my child.

No.

I refuse to believe that. There's no way my judgment is that bad, is there? There's no way she could pretend to be someone else—someone who cared about me and Isla for that long—right?

My eyes settle on a stack of articles and photos on the corner of my desk. I don't know what it is, but I'll gladly sift through it if I can stop tormenting myself with these tiresome, repetitive thoughts.

There's a note from Evan, the journalist.

Lord Greyrose, thank you again for speaking to me. I was wondering if you might be interested in sitting down for a face-to-face interview at some point soon as well. I think the public would really enjoy a look at your family's long history of being at the center of Scottish politics and business. I've included several old news clippings that we might reference during the interview. Pick the ones that you think will be interesting to talk about, and we'll go from there.

I grimace as I set the note aside. This is the kind of self-serving fluff I hate. The kind of pseudo-news I've banished to the wee hours of the morning and night on all the NewsCorp stations and affiliates.

And it's exactly the kind of fluff I need right now. I've done some serious damage to my family's reputation over the past few months, mostly thanks to my stupid, short-sighted involvement with Ella. If I can repair some of that damage with a fluff piece, I'm all for it.

I start flipping through the old newspaper clippings and see one of my parents with a man who looks familiar.

Too familiar.

Eerily familiar.

"Oh, fuck," I mutter as I squint and recognize him.

It's Max.

The same man my mother allegedly ordered to be run down.

I check the date on the article. Eleven years ago. "Christ, how long did they know the guy?"

Were they friends? They're all smiling in the photo. It's way too easy for me to imagine my mother laughing and fawning over Max while plotting his death behind his back.

Did she know about the sex tape, too? Did my father

know? Was that why they had to get rid of Max? He stumbled upon something he shouldn't have seen. So he knew way too much?

So many questions. All the plausible answers point in the same direction. Right back to my parents.

I set the photo aside and flip through the remaining articles until I find the one I'm looking for. The one with a date and a picture that places my family in New York at the same time Max was struck down and killed.

I carefully fold the photo and the article and put them in an envelope. I then write my own note and call for my assistant by pressing the intercom button.

"Get me Evan O'Connell's address, please. And call a courier. I need to have this letter delivered today. Within an hour."

My mind is reeling from everything that's happened today. Between Ella's father's surprise visit and the things I found out about my own parents, it feels like every new revelation is sicker and more twisted than the one before.

I need time and space to think, to sort out the mess I've made of my life. I don't have the luxury of taking that time anymore, though.

The first thing I have to do is get Ella out of my life. Then I have to figure out what to do about my brother and my parents.

I'm not looking forward to any of the confrontations that are looming in my immediate future, but they're all necessary. And honestly? They're all long overdue.

Ella is waiting for me in the great hall when I get back to the castle. She's changed her clothes and fixed her hair, but there's no hiding the sad, knowing look in her eyes.

"Can we talk?" she asks as I start to walk past her. "Please, Keir?"

"No," I answer, heading straight for my office. I have to

send her away, but I don't know how. I've spent the entire car ride thinking about this exact moment, but I'm still at a loss for words. "I told you this morning that I don't have anything to say to you. That hasn't changed."

I step into my office and swing the door shut behind me, but she catches it and stands in the doorway. I can feel her watching me as I put away my briefcase and turn on my computer. If she thinks I'm going to forgive her, she's wrong. If she thinks I'm going to tell her everything will be okay, she's delusional.

"You're really going to ignore me?" she asks. "Aren't you at least a little curious to hear my side of the story?"

My eyes narrow as I look across the room at her. "Will it change the basic facts? Is your side of the story somehow wildly different from what I already know? From what you've already admitted out loud?" I can hear my voice rising, but I'm powerless to stop it. "Because unless you have some new information that completely contradicts what you said this morning, I don't want to hear it."

"If I do give you more information, will you believe me?"

"Probably not." I shake my head. "But what do you expect? You've been caught in a lie, Ella. A big lie. A bad one. Did you really think I wouldn't find out eventually?" I hold my hand up when she starts to answer. "Never mind. I don't want to know. It doesn't matter."

She's starting to cry again, but how can I know that isn't part of the act? How can I trust anything she says or does ever again?

I can't. I won't.

"You have to go," I say, steeling my heart against the sight of her tears. "You can't stay here anymore."

"Where will I go?"

I shrug. "My guess would be New York, but it's not really

164

my concern anymore. As far away from me and my daughter as possible, if you're asking what I'd prefer."

"Can I at least go say goodbye to Isla?"

Fuck.

Why am I starting to feel sorry for her? She lied to Isla, too, after all. Now that I know Ella's true motives, I can't risk letting her near my daughter again. She'll probably just try to turn Isla against me.

"No. And don't contact her after you leave here. I'm serious, Ella. I'll take you to court and file charges against you if I have to."

It hurts to say those words, and I think it probably hurts her to hear them, but the time for being nice and understanding has passed. I loved her, and she betrayed me.

Now I have to cut her out of my life completely. I have to pretend like she doesn't exist.

CHAPTER TWENTY-FIVE

ELLA

Saffron is waiting in her driveway when my taxi pulls up in front of her house. "I'm sorry for all of this," I say before I can even fully get out of the car. "I didn't know who else to call."

"I'm glad you called me," she says, pulling me into a hug and helping me with my suitcase. "Do you want to talk about it now? Or do you want to rest and give me some more details later?"

"We can talk now," I say as she leads me into her thatched-roof house, which looks like something out of a fairytale. "Do you have some tea?"

"Of course." She pulls out a chair at the table for me and then quickly moves around the kitchen. "I always have tea. All day, every day."

She brings over two steaming cups and sits down next to me. "Now, have a sip, and tell me what my boneheaded brother has done this time."

I take a big drink and a deep breath, then launch into the whole, long, sordid story. I start with the first time I came to Scotland and end with the confrontation with my dad, only taking a few short breaks to dry a few fresh rounds of tears in between.

"Wow," is all she says for several long seconds when I'm finished. "I'll be honest, that's a lot crazier than I thought it would be. I assumed when you called that the two of you had just argued about… I don't even know. Normal things?" She shakes her head. "There's nothing normal about anything you just told me, though."

"I know." I stare down into the bottom of my empty teacup. "I was so stupid. I've made my share of mistakes, and I'll freely admit to them. But then Keir went and validated every single fear and bias I've had this entire time. It's not like this is the first time he's flown into a rage and sent me packing."

"Yes, that's correct," she nods, but I can tell she's unsure. "Maybe we should talk more about this later. Or in the morning. You're definitely going to stay the night here, so I won't even entertain the thought of you going somewhere else before tomorrow."

We've already spent hours talking and I'm too exhausted to argue. "Thank you. You don't know how much I appreciate this. You've always been so nice to me. You're the only one who has, really, except for Isla."

She gives me a sympathetic smile. "I'm sure you and Keir had some nice moments as well, mixed in with all that drama. "Or else you wouldn't have stayed as long as you did."

"I'd still be there now if he hadn't kicked me out. I'm not the one who ended it. I haven't ever been the first one to make that move."

"Like I said, maybe we should talk about it more later, once you've had a chance to rest."

I cock my head to the side. "Why are you holding back, Saffron? It's not like you to keep your opinion to yourself. That's one of the things I like about you."

"But will you still like it if I tell you something you don't want to hear?"

Probably not, but I nod anyway. "This is your house. You're my friend, and you know your brother better than anyone the planet. If that doesn't give you all the justification you need to speak your mind, I don't know what does."

"Maybe we should have some more tea first."

Lord, she really is avoiding the subject. She won't even look me in the eye.

I wait until she refills both our teacups and sits down again before asking her, point blank, to spill whatever it is that's on her mind. "Tell me, Saffron. I promise I won't get angry."

I hope it's a promise I can keep. Judging from the wary look on her face, I'm not so sure. I meant what I said about her being my friend, though. She's my only friend this side of the Atlantic, in fact, so I do value her opinion on most things.

She gives me one more reassuring smile and reaches over to pat my hand. "Just remember that I really do think highly of you. I would love nothing more than to see you in a relationship with my brother, okay?" She waits for me to nod, then continues. "But you keep saying you didn't end the relationship, that he kicked you out and sent you packing." After pausing to take a sip, she says, "I'm not sure you've really come to terms with your own role in all of this."

Okay, she was right. That isn't what I want to hear. "What do you mean? I understand why he's angry with me. I don't blame him for it."

"You don't blame him, but that isn't the same thing as accepting your share of the responsibility. You should have told him the truth about the plans you made with your dad. You shouldn't have made those plans in the first place, but lying about what you did and hiding it were just adding insult to injury."

Damn.

She's right again. I can't even argue with her because there's no other way to spin it. "I guess I wasn't thinking about it that way before," I admit. "Maybe he wasn't overreacting this time."

"Think of how angry you'd be if the situation were reversed. How else was he going to react?"

"Yeah, you're right. I feel awful for what I've done, but maybe it's all going to work out for the best. I couldn't have handled being his dirty little secret for much longer. I don't think he's ready for the kind of relationship I need. We just weren't meant to be."

As much as it hurts to say those words out loud, they need to be said. I have to be totally, brutally honest with myself if I'm ever going to get past this and start healing my heart.

"Maybe the two of you are meant to be," she says, frowning. "But maybe the timing is wrong. You want what he can't give. He wants what you can't give. At least you've both realized it now, before you made some kind of commitment you couldn't keep."

She's talking about marriage, and that makes my eyes well up all over again. God, I would have loved to marry Keir. If only things had gone differently.

My phone buzzes with a text, startling both of us. I reach for the phone, my heart suddenly beating wildly. Saffron is watching me. I can tell by her expression that we're both thinking the same thing.

What if it's Keir?

What will I say? Should I even read the message at all?

Okay, that's a dumb question. Of course I'm going to read it. But when I reach for my phone and squint at the screen, I see the message isn't from Keir at all. "It's a text from Isla," I say quietly, my heart breaking into a million pieces all over

169

again at the realization that I've probably seen her for the last time.

When I swipe to read the message, the tears start falling uncontrollably. Bless her heart. She didn't ask for any of this and is too young to fully comprehend the chaos that's always swirling around her.

I wish you could come back. I miss you.

I keep reading those words over and over again until I'm crying too hard to see anything at all. Saffron puts an arm around me and tells me it's all going to be okay, but I don't know if it is.

I don't know if I'll ever be okay again.

CHAPTER TWENTY-SIX

KEIR

I'm on my way to meet Saffron for lunch. It has nothing to do with the fact that Ella has been staying at her house for the past week.

Nope.

Ella has nothing to do with it.

This is just me wanting to spend some quality time with my younger sister. That's all. I'll strenuously deny any other implication.

But I do hope Ella is okay.

There.

I can admit it, at least within the privacy of my own thoughts.

Saffron is waiting for me at the table when I get to the restaurant, which is good, because I'm way too grouchy and restless these days to sit by myself for more than a few minutes at a time.

"Look at you." She smiles and stands to give me a hug. "Almost on time. I'm almost impressed."

"That's what I want to be," I say wryly as I take a seat across from her. "Almost impressive."

"So what's new?" She arches a brow and pins me with a

hard look. "I'm actually kind of surprised you accepted my invitation today."

"Because you're going to take Ella's side over your own brother?" I shoot back, unwilling to take any shit when she doesn't know all the details.

"You might be surprised to hear that I'm trying to stay impartial." She pauses long enough for us to order when the waiter stops by, then continues. "I gave Ella some pretty direct friend-talk about where I thought she messed up. She agreed with me. Well, mostly. So no, we're not over at my house plotting your downfall or anything dramatic like that."

I actually surprised to hear that Ella has accepted any responsibility for the way things ended between us, but that isn't going to change how I feel. "She's doing okay, then?" I ask because I'm fucking weak and can't help myself.

"Depends on your definition of 'okay,' I guess, but yeah. I think she'll be fine eventually. She's a strong woman who's had her heart broken, but she'll bounce back."

I nod, afraid to open my mouth again in case I say something stupid, like how much I'd been missing her or how I wish things had gone down differently that day her dad came to my house.

"Let's talk about something else," I say instead, unwilling to go too far down the rabbit hole of wishing for things that aren't ever going to happen. "What else have you been up to lately? How was your trip to America?"

"How'd you know I went to California?" her brows furrow as she sits perfectly upright in her chair. "Have you and Mom been spying on me?"

I know she's joking, but I can't stop myself from bristling at the question. "I'm not Mom. I don't spy."

I also don't arrange for people to be murdered.

"Okay, okay," she holds her hands up. "I guess I hit a

nerve. But my trip was fine, to answer your question. I spent some time with Deacon while I was there."

"Deacon? My friend, Deacon?"

"Do you know of any other guys named Deacon?" She rolls her eyes. "It's not like you have a monopoly on his time. He told me he hasn't even spoken to you since we were all in L.A. together. "That was forever ago."

"It's been a while, yeah," I grumble. "Listen to me, though. I don't want you to get involved with Deacon. He's a good guy and a great friend, but I don't want to have to knock him out for taking advantage of my sister."

She wrinkles her nose. "He didn't *take advantage* of me. Not the way, it's not any of your business. And no, I didn't go there to hook up with him, but I might take an internship at his company this summer if he has a spot for me."

"Why? You can stay here and work for free at NewsCorp if you want to be an intern."

Another eyeroll. "No offense, but there's no way in hell I want to work for you. The only internship I'm interested in taking is the one in Los Angeles. I'm not going to let you talk me out of it, so don't even try."

I clench my teeth, barely able to bite back an overly-harsh reply. "Noted," I grind out. "And no offense taken."

Our appetizers arrive, and I'm too hungry to keep bickering with my sister. I believe her when she says she won't be talked out of going to Los Angeles, but that doesn't mean I'm out of options.

I still have Deacon's number. I think it's time to finally give him a call.

"You really are an arrogant asshole," Deacon says over the speaker on my phone as I ride home from the restaurant. "Has anyone ever told you that before?"

"Only everyone who's ever met me," I snap, only half-joking. "And I might be an asshole, but I'm not fucking around, Deacon. I don't want you to date my sister. I hate the thought of having to end our friendship when you break her heart."

"You're all worked up over nothing," he assures me, but I can tell by his tone that he's probably lying. "Stella is a great girl, but I don't think it would work out between us."

"Exactly. It wouldn't. It's best not to even try."

"You are the expert on these things," he says under his breath.

"What the fuck is that supposed to mean? I'm the expert in what things?"

Deacon and I have always enjoyed teasing each other. It's usually just lighthearted, brotherly ribbing, but he's danger-ously close to crossing the line this time.

"All I'm saying is that you had a good thing going with Ella. She's a good girl. Smart, pretty, and funny. I don't know what the hell she sees in you, but I heard you were dumb enough to break things off with her. Not that I should be surprised. You've always had a knack for self-sabotage when things are going well in your life."

"Fuck you," I say, scrubbing a hand down my face as I stare incredulously at my phone screen. This conversation has gone from bad to worse. I'm pretty sure we aren't joking anymore. "I don't know where you're getting your informa-tion from, but it sounds pretty fucking biased to me."

"Is it really that biased?" he asks because he knows me too damn well. "And you know exactly where I'm getting my information from, so don't play dumb. I already told you I'm not dating your sister, but I don't think it's any secret that I've spoken to her and hung out with her more over the past few months than I have with you over the past ten years."

Damn.

Why did I call him again? Oh, right. Because I wanted to warn him that if he fucks Saffron, I'll kill him.

"Look," I exhale, trying to regain my composure even though I'm genuinely pissed. "I don't want to fight with you. I've said everything I need to say, so I'll stop lecturing you about your relationships if you agree to stop lecturing me about mine."

"I'm not trying to lecture you, buddy." The edge is gone from his tone, even though I have a feeling he's about to contradict his statement by giving me another damn lecture. "I'm just saying that from everything Saffron's told me, you fucked things up with Ella."

"She played a part in fucking things up, too," I point out, though it almost feels petty to say the words out loud.

"Maybe she did. But you're the one who can make it right. I think you should. The two of you are really good together. She's the only girl I've seen who can tolerate your nonsense for more than a week or two."

He isn't wrong about that, unfortunately. But he is wrong about the rest. It's too late to fix things with Ella. It's too late to make things right.

"I have to go," I say, suddenly feeling tired and stressed after dealing with my sister and my supposed friend all afternoon. "I'll talk to you later, Deacon. Take care."

I hang up before either of us can say anything else. I'm afraid I'll lose control of my emotions if I open my mouth again. I'm damn sure not going to let that happen.

I slump back in the cab seat and stuff my phone into my pocket. Is Deacon right? Am I being stupid? Am I throwing away the best thing that's ever happened to me? The chance to be really, genuinely happy?

Maybe.

Probably.

But what am I supposed to do? It really is too late to fix things. That's assuming I *want* to fix things.

As far as I'm concerned, that ship has sailed.

CHAPTER TWENTY-SEVEN

ELLA

It's still dark outside, and I feel like I've only been asleep for an hour or two at the most when I hear Saffron calling my name.

"How is it already morning?" I mumble to myself, raising my head to look at the clock next to my bed. My flight back to New York is leaving early, but not this early.

Except it isn't morning. Well, technically it is, since it's one o'clock in the morning. But it's definitely too early for me to be awake.

"Ella!" Saffron calls again, appearing in the bedroom doorway with her hair looking a mess and struggling with a jacket that's hanging half off her body. "I'm sorry to wake you, but I have to go. I just got a call from Keir's property manager. The castle is on fire. You might have to call a cab to get to the airport in the morning if I'm not back by then. I'm really sorry."

She disappears again before her words fully sink in. I'm still half-asleep and way too tired to fully comprehend what's going on, but I'm able to latch on to two important words she said.

Castle.

Fire.

Shit.

"Saffron!" I call after her, jumping out of bed and ignoring the way the room seems to tilt as my body rebels against the sudden movements I'm making. "Wait just one second, please. I'll come with you. I just need to throw on some clothes."

When I find her, she's in the kitchen, wearing a pair of rubber boots. "You don't have to do this," she says, throwing me a sympathetic look. "I'm not trying to put you and my brother in an awkward situation."

I make a dismissive gesture as I quickly button my pants and smooth a hand down over my wrinkled shirt. "I'm more worried about making sure Keir and Isla are okay. Plus, they'll need all the extra hands they can get to help save paintings and furniture and whatever else might be in harm's way."

"All right," she says, nodding. "You're right. Let's go."

Thank God, she isn't arguing with me. I might not be thrilled about the prospect of seeing Keir again, but I won't be able to rest until I know he and Isla are safe. I don't care how awkward it gets after that.

Just please, God, don't let anything happen to them.

The sky is orange, and I can see the flames before we make it down the long driveway to the castle. The closer we get, the worse it looks.

"My God," I murmur, my eyes going wide as the burning castle comes into view. "This is like a horror movie."

"Like a hellscape. Do you see my brother anywhere?"

I shake my head; I'm too overwhelmed to speak. There are at least a dozen people here already, but no sign of Keir.

"You go that way," she says as soon as we get out of the car, pointing to the east wing. "I'll go this way. Yell for me when you see him."

I stumble along the pebbled driveway, scanning every face I see. "Keir?" I call out, trying to tamp down the panic that's rising up inside me. "Keir? Isla?"

Where are they? Why aren't they answering?

I'm nearly in tears when I hear his voice. I can't tell what he's saying, but I'd know that deep voice anywhere.

Shit.

He's inside.

I don't stop to think. I don't call out for Saffron even though there's a little voice in my head telling me I should. I just have to get to Keir.

"Keir?" I call out again when I make it into the great hall. The cavernous space is filled with smoke. The heat is already unbearable, even though the flames don't seem to have reached this part of the building yet. "Keir, are you in here?"

"Ella?" He appears out of the smoke, covering his mouth and nose with his sleeve. "Is Isla with you?"

"No," I say as I look around, panic taking over. "Is she— you don't know where she is?" I don't wait for him to answer, I just start running toward the stairs. "Isla! Isla, honey! Can you hear me?"

I can't hear anything except sirens and yelling and my own heart beating out of my chest. I'm halfway up the stairs before Keir catches up to me, pulling me close as I start to cough.

"She isn't in her room," he yells over the chaos all around us. "I've looked everywhere. I've asked everyone, but nobody has seen her."

"You've looked everywhere?" I pull away from him, looking around wildly. "Everywhere? You're sure?"

If he answers, I can't hear him. I'm moving on instinct alone, frantic to find her as I rush down the long corridor. I don't know what makes me think to check in my old bedroom, but it's the first place I think of.

"Isla," I call out, crouching down and trying to squint through the smoke. "Isla? Are you in here?"

As soon as I open the bedroom door, I see her. She's just a little lump in the middle of the bed, her face buried in the twisted, rumpled sheets.

I scoop her into my arms, turning back toward the door and running right into Keir's broad, muscular chest. "I have her," I shout. "Help me get her out of here."

I'm feeling lightheaded and everything is a blur. I can't breathe and can hardly see more than two or three feet in front of me, but I'm trusting Keir and my own legs to get me out of here.

"This way," Keir directs me down the corridor until we reach the staircase. "Here, I'll take her." He lifts Isla out of my arms so we can move faster. "We have to hurry. I don't know if she's breathing."

I'm too shocked and scared to cry, too numb and disoriented to do anything but place one foot in front of the other, following right behind Keir until we're finally down the stairs and out the front door.

A coughing fit overtakes me as my lungs start to fill with air, but at least I can sort of see again. Keir still has Isla cradled in his arms. He's sprinting toward an ambulance. I try to follow but get intercepted by Saffron.

"Isla," I croak, my throat sore from inhaling so much smoke. "I have to check on Isla."

She follows my gaze until she spots Keir, then takes my hand and helps me run across the lawn toward him.

By the time we get to the ambulance, two emergency workers are giving her mouth-to-mouth and doing chest compressions. She looks so tiny and helpless on the gurney. All I can do is stand still and pray that she's going to be okay.

After the third round of breathing and compressions, her

small body convulses into a coughing fit that's mixed with a loud wail.

"She's alive," I say, happy tears streaming down my cheeks. "Thank God she's alive."

"Thanks to you," Keir says, kneeling down to hold her hand as she sputters and sniffles and looks around with unfocused, glassy eyes. "Can you hear me, sweetheart?"

"Is Ella here?" Her tiny voice cracks as she scans all the faces around her, finally landing on mine.

"Right here, sweetie," I say as I crouch down next to her father, dashing at the tears. "We found you in my old room. Do you feel okay? Does anything hurt?"

She shakes her head, then nods. "My head hurts. And my throat."

The EMT looks over at Keir and gives him a reassuring smile. "She's inhaled quite a bit of smoke, but it's good that she's coherent and talking. We should still probably take her to the hospital so the doctor can keep her under observation, though."

"Of course," Keir says, nodding. "Whatever we need to do." Turning back to Isla, he smiles, his own eyes bright with emotion. "We're just going to make sure you're okay on the inside, sweetheart. I'll be right there with you the whole time."

She looks over at me. "Will you be there, too, Ella?"

A pained look crosses her face as I shake my head. "I don't think there's enough room for me in that ambulance, kiddo."

She doesn't say anything else as the EMTs lift her into the back of the ambulance. Keir stands up and moves next to me, giving them more room to do their jobs. "You're welcome to follow us to the hospital if you'd like."

"I would like to," I admit. "But that'll just make saying goodbye even harder. Will you call and give us an update later, though? Once the doctors have had a chance to take a look at her?"

"I will." He glances over at Saffron, who belatedly takes a few steps back, giving us some privacy. "Thank you, Ella. I don't know what I'd do if you hadn't shown up when you did. You knew exactly where to go. It was like a miracle. "I," he pauses, choking on the final word. "I'm sorry. I thought I'd lost her. I thought I'd lost both of you. It was the worst fucking feeling in the world."

My heart hurts for him, but I've cried so much over the past several days that I don't have any tears left in my body. "She's going to be okay, though. That's the important part." I force a smile because this isn't about me or him. This is about Isla. "You didn't lose her."

He nods, then slowly exhales. "But I've still lost you, haven't I?"

God, he's killing me. I have to stay strong, though. I owe it to myself to start putting our relationship behind me. "Tonight hasn't changed anything between us. I'm just glad the two of you are okay."

"Can I take you to lunch tomorrow, at least? Just as a way of saying thank you?"

I shake my head. "I have to catch a flight back to New York in a few hours. I'm sorry, Keir." I look back over my shoulder to where Saffron is waiting. "I should go."

Without saying anything else, he turns back to Isla and I turn to Saffron.

And just like that, it's over.

We're done.

Again.

CHAPTER TWENTY-EIGHT

KEIR

Numb.

That's what I feel. Nothing at all, like I'm floating in a room temperature pool that goes on endlessly.

I sit and stare out the window at my Glasgow office, unable to focus on anything. My desk is piled high with contracts and memos. But I have turned my back on them—on all my work, really.

How am I supposed to get anything done when I feel so...

What's the word?

I struggle to string together words that form a coherent sentence. I just keep thinking about the sheer disappointment on Ella's face when she said her final words to me.

"I should go."

The memory makes me feel...

Numb.

When the door to my office slams open, I abruptly spin in my chair. A nasty rebuke is already on my lips toward the person who dared to interrupt my solitude.

But then I see Saffron striding through the door, her expression one of contempt. And that gives me pause.

What does Saffron have to be mad about, I wonder? In

the next second, Saffron tosses her long hair and fixes me with a glare.

"This is what you are doing? You let Ella go back to America just so that you could stare wistfully out the window?"

Almost of their own volition, my brows arch. "What?"

Saffron marches right up to my desk, landing her hand on it with a bang.

"You are such an unbelievable moron. You know that, right?"

I rock back in my seat, smoothing my tie, and give her a sour look.

"And what is it that I'm supposed to be doing? Ella will get over me. She's young. She's smart. She's beautiful. God knows she has talent. She's got everything going for her. If anything, you should feel sorry for *me*. I'm not as lucky."

"Do you even hear yourself when you talk?" Saffron makes a dismissive gesture. "You sound like an idiot. For God's sake, you are a frigging billionaire. And, may I add, a very handsome and clever one at that."

That gives me pause. "I'm not really interested in having my sister list my endowments, Saffron. I would rather go back to staring out the window."

She makes a sound of frustration and slaps the desk with her palm again. "Keiran! I'm trying to tell you something, you petulant child."

I shoot her a glare but remain silent. Clearly my little sister has something to get off her chest.

She leans forward over the desk, her gaze direct and intense. "Ella wanted you to tell her that you love her. She wanted to see a grand gesture, the moment where you get down on your knees and beg her to stay. I don't understand why that concept is so hard to understand. It's a bit of a mystery why you didn't just tell her that you can't live without her."

My mouth opens, but no words come out at first. I gape at Saffron.

Eventually, I come up with, "Ella wanted a grand gesture? Says who?"

"You really are the most simple-minded person. Literally every sappy movie since the beginning of time says that there has to be a grand gesture." Folding her arms across her chest, she gives me a hard look. "Why didn't you tell Ella how you feel?"

The back of my neck heats. I sit up straighter, pursing my lips. "Maybe I didn't tell her because I wanted her to be free of me. Or maybe you are just inventing things and I feel perfectly fine since Ella left."

Saffron makes a face. "Yeah, okay. That's why you have been moping around here for the past week."

"I haven't been moping. I'm just here to fill the time while Isla sees her new therapist."

"Cut the crap, Keir. I know you better than that."

I open my mouth to protest, but she shakes her head.

"No. Be serious. I see you, Keir. I know you. You're unhappy. Ella is unhappy. And you two being together would make both of those problems disappear. So why are you just staring out at the city, hoping that things will get better? When you want something, you make it happen. Isn't that what you always say?"

I muse over that for a second. "Maybe. But I have my reasons."

"Your reasons don't matter here! That's what I'm trying to tell you!"

I look her up and down. My heart wrenches in my chest.

Could Saffron be right?

Could Ella really miss me like I miss her?

Maybe none of my reasons really matter when Ella and I both desperately want the same thing.

"Saffron?"

She schools her expression. "Yes, Keir?"

"If I decided to make my grand gesture now… would you help me?"

Relief floods her face. A radiant smile appears shortly thereafter.

"Anything you need. Let's go get her."

Standing up, I awkwardly step over to my sister and then pull her into a hug. Saffron is stiff at first, but she soon accepts the embrace.

"I'm glad I have you on my side," I tell her.

"Always. I'm always on your side, big brother." She pushes me back an inch, beaming up at me. "What do you have in mind to convince Ella that you're serious?"

An image immediately swims into my brain. I give my sister a crooked smile.

"Know any good real estate agents in New York City?"

CHAPTER TWENTY-NINE

KEIR

"Right here," I say, looking out the window of the SUV as we pull up in front of the old building on the Upper West Side. "You can just let me out here on the curb. Thanks."

This is the first time I'm seeing the building in person. It's even more charming than the pictures online. It's almost identical to the dance studio from the movie we saw in Malta, with ivy climbing up the walls and the afternoon sunlight making the entire front facade glow a soft orange-pink hue.

It's perfect.

"Keir!" Kaia, Ella's best friend, beckons from the other side of the building.

"Kaia." I clear my throat. "Thanks for agreeing to meet me."

"Are you kidding? Ella has been a wreck since she got back. She hasn't slept or eaten. She has only cried over losing you. So when you called me…"

I squeeze her arm. "I'm going to try to fix what I broke. If she'll have me, that is."

"It's about damn time." She raises her right hand, jingling a set of keys. "I have the keys. Hurry! Ella is almost here."

My pulse quickens as I double-check the time on my

watch. "Already? You were supposed to keep her busy for another twenty minutes."

Kaia shrugs and gives me a sheepish grin. "You know how she is. I kept trying to distract her, but she was just getting more and more suspicious. I finally sent her on a fake errand to my mom's apartment, but that apparently isn't taking as long as I thought it would."

This is the problem with setting up an event on a different continent. I have a pretty specific vision of how I want this day to look. It's hard to trust other people with that vision.

Particularly when it's something so dear to my heart.

I find myself smiling in spite of the wrinkle in our plans. Talking about Ella is making me impatient to see her. I already know everything will be perfect when she gets here, regardless of what Kaia and I have planned.

Still, there are a few more things that I really, really hope are in place. "Have you been inside?" I ask, hoping she's come through for me. "Is everything set up?"

"It is," she says, nodding. "It looks amazing in there. She's going to love it."

"I hope so. I really do."

We walk inside, and I'm surprised at how spacious the ground floor is. I'm not sure how the floor plan will be configured in the future, but for now there's a polished wood floor that looks original to the pre-war building and a low stage set up at the far end of the large space.

"Yeah," I say, grinning as I take a look around. "This is perfect. Exactly what I've been picturing in my head. And the kids?"

"Behind the curtain," she answers, literally bouncing up and down on her toes from the excitement. "They're just waiting for our cue."

"Looks like they won't have to wait much longer." I

gesture to the front of the building, where a taxi is pulling up. "Do you want to meet her outside? I'll wait right here."

I'm grateful for the tinted windows as Kaia rushes out to the taxi. I can see everything going on out there from where I'm standing, but Ella won't be able to see me until she walks through the door.

My breath catches in my throat when I finally lay eyes on her. She's so beautiful. I could easily spend the rest of the day standing here, drinking in every detail of her face, her hair, and her incredible body.

Ella looks confused as Kaia leads her to the door. She keeps looking around and over her shoulder as if she's expecting someone to jump out at any second.

Has she somehow figured out that I'm involved? Will she be upset when she sees me?

I get my answer a few seconds later, when she walks in. She blinks a few times, no doubt letting her eyes adjust from the sunlight to the softer interior lighting.

"Oh my God," she gasps as her gaze finally settles on me. "Keir? What's going on? What is this place?"

"Do you like it?" I ask, carefully avoiding her other questions.

"It reminds me of that building we saw in the ballet movie," she smiles. "And it's even on the Upper West Side, just like the sort of place I've always wanted."

Her smile is infectious, and I can feel a lump forming in my throat as I take a step toward her. "You don't have to dream about a place like this anymore. You don't have to imagine it." I open my arms to encompass the entire space. "This is your building, Ella. Your ballet studio."

She blinks again, her mouth opening and closing without making a sound. "What?" she finally squeaks, her voice going up an octave. "Mine? But how? I don't understand." She turns to Kaia, her eyes narrowing. "I thought I was coming here for some kind of party. You told me it was your cousin's birthday."

"It is my cousin's birthday," Kaia shrugs. "But we're not going to his party."

"No," I say, laughing. "We're having a party for you, Ella. A party to celebrate your new studio and the ten million dollar grant you'll have to get everything up and running for the inaugural class of girls."

Right on cue, a dozen young girls file out onto the stage, clapping and cheering for their new ballet instructor.

"What is happening?" Ella laughs and dashes away from what I hope is a flood of happy tears. "Who are these sweet girls? I love them!"

"They're your students," I answer, beaming as I watch her incredulous reaction. "I had Kaia pick them. It looks like they're excited to get started."

There are more cheers and laughter as the girls rush down from the stage and swarm Ella like she's a rock star. This is her moment, and I love it.

I love her.

"I... oh my goodness." She takes a step closer to me once the girls have finished introducing themselves. "I seriously already love all of them. They're so sweet. And... did you say ten million dollars? Did I imagine that part? Is this all some kind of crazy, wonderful fever dream?"

"Not a dream. This is all for you. The studio, the students, the money. We brought your dream to life, darling. I can't wait to see what you do with the place."

"I don't know what to say." She swallows hard and pins me with a serious look. "Why are you doing this? I mean, I appreciate it more than I can say, but I don't understand. What prompted all of this?"

This is the moment I've rehearsed a million times over the past few weeks. But now that the moment has finally come, my mind is completely blank. I honestly can't think of a single word I've prepared. My brain has totally melted down.

So I give up on my brain and turn to my heart.

"Ella," I take her trembling hand in mine and give it a gentle, reassuring squeeze. "I know we've had our ups and downs as we've figured out how to navigate our feelings for each other. I know you're afraid of falling in love with someone unstable, someone who can't provide for you and who doesn't give you the stability that you need and crave. I've done some sh—."

I stop myself, remembering how many young ears are listening intently to every word.

"I've done a crappy job of proving I can be the kind of man you need, but I've had a lot of time to think and reflect on how I feel and what I want in life." I'm rambling. Damn it all, this is why I prepared a whole speech. Still can't remember a word of it, though.

"I want you, Ella," I say, finally getting to the point. "I'll do whatever it takes to make you happy. I can give you the stability you're looking for. I'll do a better job of communicating with you when things get stressful."

Okay, now I'm rambling again. I need to wrap this up, but her face is a mask of mixed emotions, and I can't tell what she's thinking.

"You'll work on your temper?" she asks, looking like she wants to smile but still holding back. "You won't throw me out of your house again?"

"You have my word that I'll be meek as a kitten and won't ever, ever try to throw you out again," I vow. "In fact, I've already made inquiries about adding you to the deed of my penthouse. You won't have to worry about leaving when you own half of it."

She laughs and steps closer, letting me put my arms

around her. "I don't know if you need to be meek as a kitten. Let's maybe go for something in the middle between the two extremes, hm?"

"I can do that." I kiss her forehead. "Whatever you want, sweetheart. I love you."

Every muscle in her body tenses and I realize it's the first time I've said those words out loud to her.

"You do?"

"I have for a long time," I confess. "I have known it for a while. I just wasn't sure how or if I should say it."

"You have?" Her eyes are bright with emotion as her body melts against me. "I love you, too. So, so much."

In the space of a few seconds, my whole world has become better and brighter. All because of love. All because of Ella.

CHAPTER THIRTY

KEIR

It feels like my whole world has changed for the better since the last time I spoke to Deacon. I can hardly remember the moody, broken, and lonely guy who had just ended things with the woman he loved and was acting like a complete asshole to one of his oldest friends.

Okay, maybe I can remember that guy and his struggles pretty well after all.

But I don't know that moody asshole anymore. I'm not the irritable jerk I used to be. Now it's time for me to apologize to my friend.

"Keir?" He sounds surprised when he answers the phone. "This is the second time within six months that you've called me. Did Hell freeze over?"

He really makes it hard to feel sorry for him sometimes, but I bite back a sarcastic reply and get straight to the point. "I'm calling because I owe you an apology. Probably several apologies, if I'm being honest."

"Several?" Deacon lets out a low whistle. "I'll be damned. Who are you and what did you do to my friend?"

"You're only getting one apology today," I say. "And that

one is looking less and less likely with every word out of your annoying mouth."

So I haven't completely mastered keeping my temper in check, but I am getting better. I let the first couple of smartass comments slide. And even though he really does annoy me sometimes, I'm glad he still refers to me as his friend. Maybe I didn't fuck things up too badly between us the last time we talked.

"Speaking of annoying," Deacon grunts. "Is there a reason for this call, or did you just run out of people in Scotland to harass?"

"I've already met my quota for the day, thank you." I grin despite the fact that he can't see me. "But shut up for a minute so I can get this all out. You've been a good friend to me. I can't think of anyone else I'd rather see my sister spend time with than you."

There are a few seconds of what I presume is stunned silence.

"Damn, man. Is this your way of giving your blessing to her move to L.A.?"

I scrunch up my face and exhale. I want to make things better, not worse. So I keep my voice steady.

"This is just me saying I'm sorry for how I acted before, and I hope you'll consider her for an internship this summer if you have one available."

"I know how hard it is for you to admit when you're wrong," he chuckles. "So I appreciate that you made this call. Thank you for that."

"I can admit when I'm wrong," I shoot back. "It's just that it happens so rarely."

He bursts out laughing. "Right, right. Of course. I don't know what I was thinking. But yeah, if Saffron wants to come out here for the summer, I'll find something for her to do."

He hurries to add, "Something her older brother would approve of."

There are times when I question why I've remained friends with Deacon for so long. Today isn't one of those times.

He's a good guy and a hell of a friend. I'm lucky to have him on my side. But I'll still kick his ass if he tries anything with my sister.

New York is starting to feel more and more like a place I could call home. I've always enjoyed the fast pace of life in Manhattan, but I've never really considered where I might like to live in the city until recently.

Now, with Ella, Isla. Joy in tow, I'm hoping we can all four agree on the perfect place to settle down while we're here. I don't think I'll ever give up my estate in Scotland, but it would be nice to have a base of operations in America now that we've outgrown a single hotel suite.

"What did you all think of the last place?" I ask on the elevator ride up to a penthouse overlooking Central Park. "The building was brand new with lots of fun stuff, right?"

"I liked that there was a pool on the roof!" Isla claps her hands together in excitement. "And a movie theater *way* down underneath the building."

"With about sixty floors of neighbors in between," Ella points out. "I'm curious to see this place," she says instead. "A duplex in a smaller building seems like it might be a better fit for us."

We all turn to Joy, who blushes and nibbles at her lip. "I've liked every one we've seen so far, but," she pauses for a moment. "Do you think we can get a cotton candy machine like they had in that one kitchen? That would be really cool."

Ella looks over at me and smiles. "No promises on the cotton candy machine," she says, pulling her younger sister in for a half-hug. "Our dentist would probably have a heart attack."

The elevator opens up, and we step out into the bright, airy foyer of a two-story duplex with floor-to-ceiling views of the park.

"Wow," both kids say at the same time as they run over to the window together.

The real estate agent is grinning from ear to ear as she walks in from the living room to meet us. "It looks like we have the seal of approval from two of the toughest critics," she says with a nod toward the kids. "What about the two of you? First impressions?"

I can't stop smiling as I look at Ella. "I think you might have been right about this place, baby."

"Yeah?" Her eyes are bright and full of possibilities as they dart around the room. "It's so bright and open. It feels…" She's beaming as I reach for her hand. "It feels like home."

Home.

Our first home together.

It's a damn good feeling to know that we'll both be able to put our own personal touches on this place and that our two distinct styles will overlap and mesh until it becomes something entirely new.

Something that looks like us. Both of us.

CHAPTER THIRTY-ONE

ELLA

Later, we christen the new penthouse. Isla has gone to bed. Ella is walking from the living room to the dining room, shaking her head. When she sees me leaning against the doorway of the primary bedroom, she comes over, a lot of awe still in her voice.

"I can't believe you found this place. It's beyond perfect."

"It's not the only thing that's perfect." I push off the door frame and reach out a hand to snag her tiny waist. "And I can't believe you've agreed to live here with me."

"Keir," she says, amused. "And just what exactly do you think you are doing? Hm?"

"I'm going to fuck the hell out of you so that we both remember exactly what it's like to have a perfect day," I rumble. I don't stop pushing my way through the threshold and into the shadowy bedroom until she's on the mattress.

She flexes her hips against mine, arching up to twine her arms around my neck. I allow myself to be dragged down by her weight. Burying my face in her collarbone, I grip her neckline with both hands and rip her blue dress down to the waist. I expect her to resist again, but she simply encourages me, flicking her hips into mine and letting out a hungry moan.

I press my lips into hers, kissing her as hard and as passionately as I can without drawing blood. My cock is wedged between our bodies, and one of her hands travels down my neck and along my ribs, toward my zipper.

I growl and grab her hands, jerking them up over her head. Ella is at my command in this position, at the mercy of my ravenous mouth, my heavy weight on top of her body, my cock pulsing with need. My tongue ravishing hers, my kiss harsh, I pin both of her wrists with one of my enormous hands.

I run my free hand along her contours to her outer thigh. Gentleness isn't a concern here; I ruck her dress up as hard as I can, loving how she gasps in response. I force her wrists into the mattress, pulling back to admire her lovely face.

Her hair is a mess, her cheeks are flushed, and her enticingly tiny breasts in their see-through lace bra are heaving. God, she's like a wet dream come true right now.

"Don't move your hands," I gritted. "Tell me you heard me, darling."

She licks her lips, swipes her tongue, and nods. "Yes, Keir."

Standing up, I give her a satisfied grin. I take off my jacket and necktie, then remove my shoes. As an afterthought, I take her heels off and unbutton the top few buttons on my shirt.

She squirms little as I squat between her knees, staring down at her shredded clothing and the bits of her body I've exposed.

Looking her in the eye, I tear the final portion of her dress and undo the front clasp of her bra. Her breasts are released, and I take some time to appreciate them, reaching down and feeling the weight of them in my hands. Ella arches up into my touch, and I reward her by lowering my mouth to her breast, teasingly licking my way around it before scraping it with my teeth.

She moans, her hands reaching down to bury themselves in my hair. I release her nipple and nip the side of her breast hard. Her entire body shudders as she exclaims, "ow!"

"Put your hands back up over your head," I order her.

Ella blinks a few times before biting her lip and slowly raising her hands above her head. I drop a kiss in between her breasts, groaning a little.

"Good girl," I murmur against her hot skin.

My cock throbs as I lower my body down, hooking my fingers in the waistband of her small thong. I glide her underwear down her thighs, burying my nose in the warm heat of her legs just below her pussy. She's already wet, as evidenced by the stain on her pants and the earthy but pungent aroma of her pussy rising to my nostrils.

When I pull back, she whimpers. Her pleading shows genuine desperation. "Keir…"

I smirk down at her, unbuttoning the rest of my shirt and slipping it off. Ella squirms again, her hazel eyes clouded with want.

I lean down and kiss her lips again, my hands gripping her hips. "What is it, sweetheart?" I whisper against her soft lips.

Her hips dig into mine as she thrusts. "I need more."

Hearing her innocent cry makes me want to remove my pants and bury my cock so deep inside her pussy that I might never find my way out. But I'm trying to take it slow, so I just kiss her hard, pressing my tongue against hers.

When she screams and writhes against me, I pull back and inspect her face. "I'm going to take my time with you, love. The longer you wait for me to fuck you for the first time, the more explosive it will be. And I have all the time in the world... so I'm not going to pop your cherry tonight. I'm going to make you wait a little longer before I help you come, sweetheart."

Her air is expelled from her lungs with a soft groan. I notice her hands flexing. "Keir..."

I stand up and remove my slacks, leaving me nude underneath. Ella raises her hips, her gaze fixed on my shaft. She takes a deep breath and lets out a tiny groan.

I bite my lower lip and drag my palm down to my groin, drawing big circles around my cock. I gaze down at Ella's gorgeous figure stretched out in front of me.

"Spread your legs for me, sweetheart," I say. "Show me what I'm missing."

Her face heats up, but she looks so fucking hungry as she slowly spreads her knees wide, exposing her creamy pussy. I run my free hand inside her thigh, up to her pussy lips. She hisses and shakes her hips against the brush of my fingertips. I circle her entrance a few times, gathering the sticky fluids I find there.

"Does that feel good, sweetheart?"

"Yes," she whimpers. "Yes, God."

I fist my cock, staring at her pussy, wet from its own juices. My dick is so sensitive from all this buildup that I know I won't last long. So I focus on Ella, on driving her over the edge.

I run my fingertips up, distributing the liquid I've discovered around her clit. She closes her eyes and hisses as I make slow figure eights around her clit and her entrance.

"Bring one of your hands down here," I order her. "I want to watch you touch yourself, sweetheart. I want to see the pleasure on your face."

Her eyes open, piercing me through, as she draws one shaky hand down the length of her body. Her fingers brush across mine as she caresses her clit. She starts to close her eyes again, a small mmm coming from the back of her throat.

"Use your other hand to feel your tits," I advise.

She grabs her breast and twists it around. A shudder of ecstasy shocks her little frame. I hold my cock and pump it a few times. Then, with the other hand, I run my fingers down to her pussy entrance.

I fix my gaze on her. "Look at me, Ella. I want to see your reaction when I make you come with my fingers."

Her eyes open, pinning me in place. Her thick lips part as I tease her entrance. She's slippery with want, making it easy to slip one thick digit inside the warmth of her body.

Her expression changes from one of delight to one of pain. I'm afraid I've hurt her. But then she starts sliding her fingers in little circles around her clit.

My body tightens with yearning. I attempt to keep my grasp on my cock light, but my hand is already massaging my dick. It throbs in my hand, but I'm trying to get Ella to the breaking point before I spill my seed all over her gorgeous body.

Her hips thrust as she bites her bottom lip. "Give me more," she urges, her voice seductive. "Fuck, Keir..."

I move my hand so that my palm faces upward and introduce a second big finger to her tight pussy. As I carefully stroke my fingers in and out of her channel, I can feel the walls starting to shake.

"Oh god," she breathes. "Oh god..."

"I want to see you unravel, Ella," I utter.

She starts coming as soon as her gaze settles on my face, her core muscles spasming. Her lower body convulses, and her eyes roll up in the back of her skull. She lets out a choking sound that is like music to my ears.

"Fuck, Ella," I grit out.

Only a few seconds later do I feel my balls pull up and

my cock begin to quiver. I shoot hot pulses of semen across her thighs and belly, my eyes closing briefly as I come so hard that it almost aches. I hear an odd sound and then realize it's a low sigh leaving my chest. I feverishly thrust a couple more times, draining out every last drop of pleasure in my body.

I can't speak as I open my eyes and sink into the mattress alongside Ella. She wraps herself around me, seeking my mouth, and I kiss her with leisurely flicks of my tongue.

I close my eyes and let myself drift, my arm surrounding Ella's waist, my nose buried in her honey-scented hair.

CHAPTER THIRTY-TWO

KEIR

Ella is already sitting at the dining table with her laptop open in front of her when I walk into the room.

"You're sure you want to do this right now?" I ask. "You don't want to have breakfast first? Or maybe a relaxing massage? Burn some sage?"

"Don't make me laugh," she says, her lips twitching. "I have to mentally prepare myself for whatever craziness is about to go down."

We've been staying in our favorite Manhattan hotel suite for the past several days. Ella has decided today is the day we should set some boundaries with her out-of-control father.

I'm not convinced it's a good idea after our last encounter with him, but I'm going along with it because I'll be damned if I let Ella deal with him alone.

We're a team now.

Partners.

"I'll let you do most of the talking," I say, reaching for her hand under the table as I sit down next to her. "If you need me to jump in, all you have to do is squeeze my hand. And if he starts getting too nasty, we can just end the call. You don't have to put up with his abuse anymore, baby. Not ever."

"I know." She smiles and presses the button on the laptop to connect the video call. "I'm glad you're here with me."

"Always." I lean over to kiss her cheek just as her father appears on the screen. It's hard not to scowl at the man who caused so much conflict between me and Ella, but I promised her I'd work on my temper, and this is going to be my first big test.

If I can get through this video call without yelling, I can handle anything.

"Did you call to apologize?" are the first words out of her father's mouth.

God, please give me the strength to deal with this asshole.

"No," she answers, her tone neutral but firm. "I'm calling to let you know that I'm not going to be a part of your schemes anymore. You and I are going to have some new boundaries if we're going to have any kind of relationship moving forward."

This is the moment of truth, the moment where the conversation could go very right or very wrong. I genuinely have no idea how he's going to react to this new, assertive Ella.

But I'm eager to find out. And just for the record, I really like this confident, in-charge side of her. Then again, I like every side of her.

Unsurprisingly, her dad isn't happy. "You have a lot of nerve talking to me like that. You think that you're all high and mighty now that you're shacked up with your rich boyfriend, don't you? Well, let me tell you something, young lady. You aren't special. He'll get tired of you and move on sooner or later, mark my words."

Nope.

She might be taking the lead in this conversation, but that doesn't mean he gets a free pass to be a jerk.

"You're wrong," I say, simply. "About a lot of things, I'd

imagine, but definitely about that. I'm not ever going to get tired of your daughter. I won't ever leave her."

Ella looks over at me and offers a tiny smile before returning her attention to the screen in front of us. "Keir and I love each other. We're going to get married someday soon. I'd like for you to be there, but..."

"I won't be there if you keep acting like a spoiled brat," he interrupts.

"But," Ella says, raising her voice just enough to be heard over him. "I'm done letting you make demands. I'm not looking for your approval anymore, Dad. I'm not asking for it, and I don't need it."

"And just who do you think is going to walk you down the aisle? I'll bet you'll need me for that."

He really doesn't get it, does he? He can't fathom a world where his daughter won't continue putting up with his bull-shit, but he's about to find out the hard way what I've known for a while—that Ella is strong enough to make it on her own when she has to.

She's also stubborn enough to make sure she succeeds.

"I'm not worried about who will or won't walk me down the aisle," she says, giving my hand a slight squeeze.

That's my signal.

"We probably won't have a big, flashy wedding anyway," I add. "We've talked about doing something small and inti-mate, with just a few friends and family there to celebrate with us. We want to do something that will be special and meaningful for the two of us most of all." I look over at her and smile. "I'm going to do things right this time. It's going to be our day, celebrating our love for each other."

Ella's dad shakes his head, a look of disgust spreading across his face.

"You two have it all figured out, don't you? You think you have all the answers. Just wait until things get hard. Neither one of you has had to deal with real problems or do a day of real work in your pampered, spoiled lives." He grunts and mutters something under his breath, then adds, "I have to sit around and listen to my oldest daughter disrespect me while she flies all over the world with a man who is almost my age. Have you considered how that makes me feel? Just once, have you thought of anyone but yourself, Ella?"

"I, um..." She swallows hard and squeezes my hand again. "I never meant to upset you or disrespect you. My relationship with Keir doesn't reflect on you and doesn't have anything to do with you, Dad."

"By God, it does!" he shouts before I have a chance to jump in. "Everything you do reflects on me. Every bad decision you make. Every failure. That goddamn sex tape! Is it any wonder that I had to pretend your sister was sick? I needed something to deflect all the negative attention. And you still haven't sent us the money you promised. I'm starting to think you're only going to be happy when you see Joy and your mother out on the street. Is that what you want, Ella? Because I'll do it. I'll throw both of them out on their asses right now."

This conversation has gone completely off the rails. I don't know if there's any hope of salvaging it at this point.

Ella's mouth is hanging open, completely speechless. She isn't even squeezing my hand anymore.

It's way past time for me to say something. "If you kick them out, we'll fly them out here to stay with us. We'll take them back to Scotland. I have plenty of spare bedrooms."

"You can't take Joy," he barks. "You've already ruined my oldest daughter's reputation. I won't let you get anywhere near my youngest."

"He didn't ruin me," Ella fires back. "And you can't stop me from taking care of Joy. Someone clearly needs to."

"I'll call the police the minute she walks out this door," he rages. "I'll have you arrested for kidnapping if you even think about putting her on a plane."

I lean in closer to the screen so I can make sure he hears every word I'm about to say. "You won't say a word, do you understand? If you want any money at all, you'll shut your mouth right now and listen."

To my surprise, he actually does shut up. Damn, if only I'd known it was that easy. I could have saved us all a lot of hassle.

"I'm listening," he growls. "What are your terms?"

Ella looks over at me, wide-eyed. We haven't really discussed this part, so I'm just going to wing it. I give her hand a gentle squeeze this time. "I'm willing to give you a one-time, lump sum payment of twenty thousand dollars in cash. In exchange, you'll give up your parental rights and give Ella full custody of Joy."

He looks away from the screen for a moment. I can hear a woman's voice saying something. "Fifty thousand," he counters when he turns back to face us. "That's the number we'll accept."

I give Ella's hand one more squeeze, then casually shrug my shoulders. "I think we're done here. My offer is only good for the duration of this call. If we have to discuss this another time, the number will be fifteen thousand."

I reach for the keyboard, exaggerating my movements so there's no way he can mistake what I'm doing.

"Wait, wait!" he waves me off just before I hit the button to disconnect the call. "I'll… accept your offer. Twenty thousand. Cash."

"Good choice," I say, smiling. "I'll send a plane for Joy and a briefcase full of hundred dollar bills. We'll be in touch again soon."

I end the call this time without waiting for him to open his big mouth again. Ella looks like she's in shock for a moment, then she slowly starts to smile. Her smile turns to a laugh. We're standing up and falling into each other's arms in a matter of seconds.

"I can't believe that worked," she says, nearly crying from laughing so hard. "You were amazing. Watching you negotiate was kind of hot, if I'm being honest."

"Hell, you can start sitting in on the NewsCorp board meetings if it turns you on to seeing me negotiate. I'll start wheeling and dealing every damn day."

She laughs harder, releasing all those pent-up emotions and anxieties as we hold each other tight.

The call with her dad couldn't have gone any better. Twenty grand is a small price to pay if it means we don't have to deal with his shenanigans anymore. And if he ever does want to reach out and have a semi-normal relationship with either of his daughters someday, he'll know where to find them.

With me.

CHAPTER THIRTY-THREE

ELLA

The past month has been a complete blur, but in the best possible way. I've been flying back and forth from New York to Glasgow to oversee the renovations to the dance studio. Joy and Isla have been attached at the hip. Keir has actually managed to set aside time for all of us every day, even though he's also been busy with work and the restoration of Drummond Castle.

All in all, we've been happy. And it's been really nice.

This isn't quite how I pictured my perfect fairytale romance, but that's okay. It's actually better in a lot of ways.

There are still some things we have to decide, like a date for the wedding and where we're going to live since our little family has already almost outgrown the Glasgow penthouse and the castle will likely be out of commission for at least another year or more.

But overall, there's nothing I'd change. I wake up every morning with a smile on my face and the love of my life by my side. What more could I ask for?

Even now, as Saffron and I pick up the toys that Isla and Joy seem to have left all over the penthouse, I can't help but smile.

"You've been so happy lately," she says, mirroring my grin. "I like seeing you like this."

"It's a nice change of pace, isn't it?" I shoot her a knowing glance as I think back to how she helped me during the darkest part of my short-lived breakup with Keir. "At least you don't have to deal with me moping around and crying anymore."

"Amen to that," she winks. "But all jokes aside, I'm really happy for you. For both of you. And if he ever acts like a jerk again, you know exactly where to find me."

"He won't," I say, knowing it's true. "Not saying everything is sunshine and roses one hundred percent of the time, but it's not anything like it was before, either. We've both grown and changed for the better, I think. I'm proud of Keir. He's really put in the effort to make this work."

As if on cue, his voice echoes through the foyer. "Did I hear someone taking my name in vain?" Keir walks up behind me and kisses the side of my neck. "I hope it's all good things, at least."

"Definitely all good," I say, blushing as his hands move over my body.

"Easy, you two," Saffron wrinkles her nose. "I just ate. And I'm pretty sure there are a couple of impressionable kids running around."

I hold up a random stuffed animal. "They're here somewhere. They've left a trail of evidence."

Keir plucks the toy from my hand and sets it aside. "You should let the household staff take care of that stuff, darling. That's why we hired the second housekeeper." He gives me a sideways look. "Or did you give her the day off again?"

"I just feel bad when it seems like we're making their jobs harder than they need to be. There's nothing wrong with Joy's arms and legs. She can come out here and pick up her toys."

"Isla can, too," he grins. "But that still doesn't explain why you and Saffron are the ones picking up the toys."

"He does have a point," Saffron shrugs, tossing a princess doll over her shoulder. "Let's make the kids pick up after themselves while we go do something fun."

"Yes. Anything your heart desires. Hell, after being in divorce court in Scotland, almost anything else seems like a dream."

I squeeze his arm. "I'm sorry. I know that has to be a drag."

"It is. Did you know that having money actually makes the issues of divorce and custody more contentious, not less? Kinsley is trying to drag my name through the mud and make me miserable."

Saffron pulls a face. "I could see how a few million either way might make everything more complicated, yes."

"Aww." I kiss his cheek. "Soon enough, you'll be free of her."

"And ready to remarry." Saffron gives me a meaningful look.

"Okay. That's my cue to change the subject," I say. I shoot Saffron a long glance, trying to communicate that she's not being helpful right now. Keir sees the looks between us and fidgets, uncomfortable.

I could kick Saffron for that.

Thank god, in the next second, we're saved by the literal bell. The chime from the private elevator makes us all turn and look as Keir's parents step into the foyer.

"Damn," Keir grumbles, pulling me in close as he turns to face them. "Please come in," he calls out, then adds, "Oh, I guess you already have."

"We tried calling," his mother grumbles. "Several times."

Saffron moves over next to us and gives her parents a funny look. "Do you always drop by Keir's apartment unannounced? Is this why you're always trying to get me to move to the city?"

Her father makes a dismissive gesture. "Not now, Saffron. We're here because of an emergency." Turning to Keir, he nods toward the office. "Can we speak to you in private, son?"

"This isn't a convenient time for me," Keir says, shocking all of us. "You'll have to say whatever it is in front of Saffron and Ella."

"Not me," Saffron says as she begins walking toward the elevator. "I'm out of here. Call me later, Ella. We still need to go out and do something fun."

I look up at Keir as everyone else says goodbye to Saffron. "Do you want me to leave you alone with your parents for a few minutes? I don't want to intrude if it's something private."

"You aren't intruding, my darling." He presses a kiss to my forehead. "They're the ones who barged in here unannounced with some kind of supposed emergency. That's the definition of intruding."

His mother is glaring at us, but it's his dad who is doing most of the talking for a change. "Stop making all those rude comments over there, Keiran," he huffs. "We came here to get your help. You need to get on the phone with someone at the police station immediately."

"Is that what I *need* to do?" he smirks. "And here I thought I was getting too old to be told what I needed to do by my father." He pauses, then adds, "In my own home."

"I told you to stop with the rude comments. They're trying to arrest your mother, for God's sake. Someone needs to be held accountable!"

My mouth falls open, but Keiran doesn't seem to be surprised at all. "Sounds like Mother is going to be held accountable," he says, nearly sending his father into cardiac arrest.

Even his mom looks uncharacteristically worried. "You don't mean that," she gasps. "You wouldn't dare let them arrest me. Think of how that would look."

Again, Keir doesn't seem bothered. "You should have thought about how that would look before you conspired to commit murder."

Pure fury flashes in her eyes. "We'll cut you out of the will. You and your brother. His campaign is already on its last legs, so I guess you'll both be out there floundering together. We'll see if you learn some humility when you have to come begging us to pay your bills."

I've seen some pretty intense arguments between Keir and his family since I've been here, but nothing compares to what I'm witnessing now.

Not only is it the first time I've seen Keir's mother lose an argument, but it's also the first time I've seen a look of genuine fear on her haughty, aristocratic face.

"Do you understand just how much trouble you're in?" Keir asks. "I know you're not used to hearing this, but you're screwed."

His dad nods, frowning. "The family lawyer said we need to hire a criminal attorney."

"Exactly," Keir says. "You'd be smart to follow his advice. In the meantime, you don't need to worry about James. He'll land on his feet after the campaign. NewsCorp takes care of our family."

His mother snorts. "Since when?"

"Since now." Keir's voice turns from sarcastic to stern so quickly that it even makes me jump. He pulls me in closer and rests a hand against the small of my back, making sure I'm taken care of even while he's going back and forth with his parents. "Since I realized there are more important things in life than acquiring money and manipulating the people we're supposed to love the most."

Wow.

Shots fired.

If this was a soap opera, I'd be sitting on the edge of the couch by now. But it's so much more intense when it's happening right in front of my eyes, right in the middle of our living room.

Keir's dad holds his phone up and squints to read an incoming message. "Oh, no," he mumbles, the color draining from his face as his shoulders sag forward. "No, no, no. This can't be happening."

"What is it?" Keir's mom asks, leaning over to read over his shoulder. "No. They can't do that. I refuse." She looks over at Keir. "The police are here. Downstairs in the lobby. They're going to arrest me, Keiran. They're going to take me away in handcuffs."

He takes a deep breath, then slowly exhales. "I'm sorry to say you've brought this on yourself. There's nothing I can do to help you now."

His dad sputters and fumbles to put his phone away as she stomps off to the elevator. "What about me?" he asks, though I'm not sure if he's talking to his wife or his son.

Keir answers first. "You'd better start thinking about yourself and what your needs are going to be. Because mother will almost certainly spend a long, long time in prison." He waits until they're both on the elevator and the doors are closing before adding, "Oh. I really would look into hiring that criminal attorney. You're going to need all the help you can get."

The doors close on them, seamlessly ending that entire chapter of our lives. I clutch my chest, finding myself suddenly able to breathe more freely again.

Can it really be so easy? I pull Keir close, needing to feel the reassurance of his touch.

"Wow," is the first word I say after they leave. "That was the craziest, most intense thing I've ever experienced. And I saw some crazy stuff while I was working for you."

He smiles, but it fades just as quickly. "Was I too hard on her? Should I try to do something? I could probably pull a few strings and make a few phone calls to help her out."

This feels like one of those times when I should probably keep my opinion to myself. "That's totally up to you," I say, tipping my head back so he can capture my mouth in a long, deep kiss. "I think you'd be justified either way. But like you said, she brought it on herself. And what did she get out of it?"

"Arrested."

"That's right."

I don't say anything else because I don't think I need to. Like Keir said earlier, she brought it on herself. Now she's getting what she deserves.

CHAPTER THIRTY-FOUR

ELLA

Epilogue

Fiji is literally paradise. I could happily spend months right here on the beach with the man I love, the crystal clear water lapping at our feet as we talk, laugh, and kiss.

It felt a little strange to wake up the first day and not immediately reach for my phone or look at my calendar to see what I had planned for the day, but it didn't take long to get used to the feeling of being totally, completely free.

"I wish we could stay here forever," I sigh happily as we stretch before our jog along the beach. "Maybe when we're ready to retire and nobody cares if we disappear from the face of the earth for months at a time."

He laughs, pulling me in for a quick kiss. "Maybe then, my love. For now, let's enjoy every minute together."

The past six months have been the happiest in my life. Now that we're finally married, it truly feels like the happy ending to my own personal fairytale. Except it isn't an ending at all. This is just the beginning of our lives together. I'm so thankful I get to share it with Keir.

"We might not be able to jog as fast as normal," I say

215

once we've finished stretching. "I mean, it's probably fine if we do, but…"

He cocks his head to the side and gives me a curious look. "Are you okay, baby? Is your stomach upset? We don't have to jog at all if you're not feeling up to it. I'd be just as happy to lie around in bed with you."

It feels like dozens of butterflies have come to life in my stomach and are currently doing backflips as I reach down into my beach bag and pull out a small black and white photo. "This isn't how I imagined I'd tell you, but I can't hold it in anymore."

His brow furrows as he looks down at the picture in my hand. "What is it, beautiful? Whatever it is, you know I won't be upset."

I laugh as I pass the photo to him. "No, I don't think you'll be upset at all."

"What am I looking at?" He squints, turning the photo sideways, then upside down. It takes a few seconds, but I can see the flash of recognition in his eyes when he finally real-izes what it is. "Holy shit." He looks from the picture to me. "Ella, is this… are you serious? Are you sure? Is this what I think it is?"

I nod, looking up at him through my lashes, as the butter-flies start to calm down. "I'm pregnant. We're going to have a baby."

"We're going to have a baby!" he calls out, scooping me into his arms and spinning me around before stopping abruptly and gingerly setting me back on my feet. "I'm sorry, baby." His hand moves down to my belly. "I didn't hurt anything, did I? Is everything still okay in there?"

I can't help but laugh in spite of the worried look on his handsome face. "The baby is fine. We're fine. Better than fine. We're perfect."

He grins and kisses me, holding me tight in his arms as

we sway back and forth in the island breeze. "Have you told anyone else yet? Kaia, Joy, or Isla? Saffron?"

"Not yet." I love how excited he is. I knew he'd be happy, but seeing his reaction has made my heart feel full. "I figured we could sit the kids down together and tell them. And I think this will be a good excuse to bring Kaia on full-time at the dance studio. Maybe as a partner. I'd love for her to have the kind of stability in her life that I have in mine."

"I think that's a great idea," he says, nodding, still holding me as he looks into my eyes. "Have I told you how happy you make me?"

"I'm pretty sure I've heard you say something like that before." I toss him a playful wink. "Maybe once or twice."

"Once or twice?" he laughs. "That means I need to make up for lost time. You make me happier than I've ever been, baby. Happier than I would have thought was possible less than a year ago. My life is so much better with you in it. "Now," his eyes light up with emotion as his hand skims down to my belly once more. "Now you're carrying our child. A part of both of us. You've already made all my dreams come true, Ella. I'm so glad I get to share my life with you."

And now I'm crying. I don't even try to stop the happy tears from streaming down my cheeks, though. I'm too busy kissing my husband. The love of my life. The man I'm going to spend forever with. The father of my child.

"All my dreams have come true, too," I whisper. "All because of you."

CHAPTER THIRTY-FIVE

KEIR

Epilogue

My phone buzzes with the text I've been waiting for from Ella's friend, Kaia.

We're on our way. I'll be dropping her off in ten minutes.

My heart rate instantly doubles, and I think I'm starting to sweat, but I'm panicking too much to notice.

I shouldn't be nervous. I know Ella is going to enjoy the evening I've planned, but it's not enough that she just enjoys it.

This is our one year wedding anniversary.

I want her to *love* it.

Tonight has to be perfect.

And now I have nine and a half minutes to make sure nothing is going to go wrong. I start rushing from room to room in the apartment, checking and double-checking that everything is in place.

Dinner is on the table. That's a good start. I've used her favorite china, the set we got as a wedding gift from her aunt, along with some cutlery and silver that's been passed down for generations in my family.

There's music playing softly from the speakers in the living room, just loud enough to hear it in the background without being too intrusive.

Check and check.

The kids are off at one of their friends' houses for the weekend, so there is no need for us to worry about keeping our voices down or taming whatever wild, crazy urges we might have after dinner.

Big check.

I'm not sure if it's comical or sad that this is the first time in my adult life I've prepared a gourmet meal for two, with candles and music and all the little details that I wouldn't normally even notice or think of.

Is this really a thing that people do for their anniversaries?

I hope so, because it's too late to change anything now. If I can pull this off, though, it's going to be really special.

I check my watch and silently curse myself for not paying more attention when Kaia sent that text. How long has it been? Do I have five minutes left before she gets here? Four?

Dammit.

Just breathe.

Relax.

She's going to love everything.

Even if she doesn't, it'll still be perfect because we'll be together.

My pep talk could use some work, but there's no time to psych myself up any more than I already am.

Jesus, I need to get myself together. I don't think I was this nervous on our wedding day. But it feels like the stakes are so much higher now. She's six months pregnant and has had to start cutting back on some of the things she enjoys most in life, like dancing and teaching, and bending at the waist.

I just want her to be able to sit back, smile, and have a nice time without being uncomfortable or worrying about anything else for a few short hours.

Another text makes me jump, and I'm glad nobody else is around to hear the embarrassingly high-pitched noise that just escaped from the back of my throat.

I just dropped her off at the door. She's on her way up.

Oh shit. She's at least three minutes early.

That's fine, though. Totally fine. Everything is ready. Nothing is going to go wrong. I'm definitely not going to fuck anything up.

Please, God, don't let me fuck anything up.

The closest thing to a prayer I have time for right now, because I can hear the elevator door opening in the foyer and the click, clack, click of her shoes on the marble floor.

"Keir?" she calls out. "I'm home, baby."

I step into the living room to meet her with a hug and a kiss, loving the way her round belly presses against me when I hold her close.

That's our child growing inside her. The baby we made together. It might not be the first time I've experienced this particular miracle of life, but it's the first time I'm getting to experience it with Ella, and that makes all the difference in the world.

"You look beautiful," I say, meaning it as I pull away just far enough to look into her eyes. Her hair is pulled up, leaving her graceful neck exposed. The short, beaded black dress she's wearing is shimmering in the soft candlelight and hugging every curve of her lush, gorgeous body. "Happy anniversary, sweetheart."

A slow, sexy smile spreads across her pretty face. "Happy anniversary to you, too. What are we going to do

220

tonight? It's so rare that we have the apartment all to ourselves."

"Oh, I can think of a few things we could do," I say, trying and failing to sound nonchalant, as if I haven't spent the last few hours having a full-blown meltdown. "Are you hungry?"

"Starving. I kept trying to get Kaia to stop for something to eat, but she was like a drill sergeant, running me from place to place." She stops following me through the apartment and looks around, her eyes growing wide. "Did you do all of this yourself? The candles? The music? And whatever that delicious smell is?"

"That'll either be the garlic bread or the chicken piccata." I wince. "Unless it's a burnt smell, and that would be the first batch of chicken picatta. I might need to buy a new pan, but we don't have to talk about that right now. But yes, everything was prepared by me. With love, of course."

Her mouth falls open when we step into the dining room and she sees everything laid out on the table. "My goodness, babe. You really outdid yourself. I didn't have any idea you could cook like this." She walks over to the table and gasps. "And you're using the pretty china my aunt gave us! I love all of this so much, Keir. This is so beautiful and thoughtful."

"For my beautiful, thoughtful wife," I say, walking up behind her and leaning in to plant a trail of kisses up the side of her neck. "Let me pull the chair out for you, baby. All you have to do tonight is relax and enjoy. You've been running yourself ragged lately for our little family, and I want you to know I've noticed it and I appreciate everything you do. Always."

"Oh, my goodness," she laughs, dabbing at the edges of her eyes. "You're going to make me cry and mess up my makeup if you keep saying things like that."

"Well, there's just one more thing before we start eating."

221

I walk over and grab a chilled bottle from the ice bucket on the corner of the table. "I know sparkling grape juice leaves a lot to be desired, but I promise we can have a toast with actual champagne next year."

Her smile is radiant as she reaches down and absently cups her hand around her pregnant belly. "Guess our timing was a little off, wasn't it? A few months earlier or later, and we could have been drinking tonight."

"Our timing was perfect," I say, pouring each of us a glass of the cheap, bitter juice. "I'd rather drink ten bottles of this stuff than change one single thing about the past year of our lives."

She laughs. "I'm not sure if I'm just emotional tonight or if that was actually really sweet. We aren't going to drink ten bottles of this stuff, though, just for the record."

"Just one sip is all that's technically required for the toast," I toss her a wink as I raise my glass. "Ella, my love, I think you know how happy you've made me over the past year that we've been married."

"You've mentioned it once or twice," she says, nibbling at her lip as her cheeks flush a delicious shade of dark rose.

Damn, she's perfect.

"This is our first anniversary together," I continue. "The end of our first year as a married couple. But it's just the beginning of so many more happy years, and I'm truly lucky that I get to spend those years with you. Having you and Joy here has made my life and Isla's life so much better in so many ways, and I'm so thankful that God, fate, or the universe kept bringing us together no matter how many times I foolishly sabotaged our relationship in the beginning. I didn't realize I was so close to messing up the best thing that's ever happened to me, but I'm glad you never gave up on me." I reach over to clink my glass against hers. "This is to you, for your grace and understanding."

"To us," she whispers, her eyes suspiciously bright with emotion. "And to never giving up."

It took a few false starts and stops, but we made it. We're happier after this first year than we've ever been, and our love is growing stronger every day.

Soon, our little family will grow a little bigger, and the love in our hearts will grow right along with it.

I can't wait.

CHAPTER THIRTY-SIX

Do you love Keiran and Ella's story? There is a little bit more ooey-gooey epilogue for just for you! Get an extended epilogue right now by joining Vivian's mailing list.

ABOUT VIVIAN WOOD

Vivian likes to write about troubled, deeply flawed alpha males and the fiery, kick-ass women who bring them to their knees.

Vivian's lasting motto in romance is a quote from a favorite song: "Soulmates never die."

Be sure to join her email list to keep up with all the awesome giveaways, author videos, ARC opportunities, and more!

Vivian's Works

Married At Midnight Series - coming 2023
Forbidden Billionaire Romance
Deal With The Devil
Wed to the Devil
Vow to the he Devil

Ruined castle series
Forbidden Billionaire Romance
The Scottish Billionaire
The Beast
The nanny
The caress

Broken Slipper series
Forbidden Billionaire Romance
The Patron
The Dancer
The Embrace
Possessive

Ravaged Dream Series - coming 2023
Forbidden Billionaire Romance
The Rogue
The Intern
The Secret

Dirty royals
Forbidden Royal Romance
The Royal Rebel
The Wicked Prince
His Forbidden Princess
Royal Fake Fiancé

Lyon Dynasty world
Dark Billionaire Romance
King's Capture
Queen's Sacrifice

Sinfully rich series
Steamy Billionaire Romance

SINFUL FLING
SINFUL ENEMY
SINFUL BOSS
SINFUL CHANCE
SINFULLY RICH

HIS AND HERS SERIES
HIS BEST FRIEND'S LITTLE SISTER
CLAIMING HER INNOCENCE
HIS TO KEEP
HIS VIRGIN

THE ADDICTION DUET
ADDICTION
OBSESSION

OTHER BOOKS
WILD HEARTS

For more information....
vivian-wood.com
info@vivian-wood.com